reasonable doubt

VOLUME THREE

VOLUME THREE

WHITNEY G.

This is a work of fiction. Names, characters, places, and incidents either are the product of the author's imagination or are used fictitiously, and any resemblance to actual persons, living or dead, business establishments, events, or locales is entirely coincidental.

Cover designed by Najla Qambers of Najla Qambers Designs
http://najlaqamberdesigns.com/

ISBN-10: 1500985783
ISBN-13: 9781500985783

For my BFF/ultimate beta-reader/amazing assistant/ shoulder to cry on whenever I'm acting crazy/ "person" like they say on 'Grey's Anatomy'...Tamisha Draper. (My books would suck without you...)

To Tiffany Neal. Thank you for being the balance. You'll always be the perfect balance...

To Natasha Gentile...How did you become my friend? LOL

And for the F.L.Y. crew: I fucking love you more than you'll ever know...

table of contents

prologue

Several months ago…

Andrew

It was all there in black and white, front and center, no filler. Although the facts were skewed and *The New York Times* had once again neglected to post my photo, the damage to my firm—Henderson & Hart, was now done. And I knew exactly what was about to occur, step by step.

I'd seen it happen in this city too many times before.

First, the top clients who'd sworn to always stay by my side would call and say that they "suddenly" found new representation. Then the employees would file letters of resignation—knowing that having a tainted firm on their resumes would hinder their careers. Next, the investors would call—pretending to sympathize as they publicly denounced me in the media and promptly pulled all funding.

Last, and most unfortunately, I was sure to become another hotshot lawyer who ruined his career before it could even begin.

"How much longer do you think you'll be able to get away with stalking Emma?" The private investigator I hired stepped beside me.

"She's my fucking daughter. I'm not stalking her."

"Five hundred feet." He lit a cigarette. "That's how far you're supposed to be."

"Are they treating her right during the week?"

He sighed and handed me a stack of photos. "Private preschool, early tap-dance lessons, and weekends at the park as you can clearly see. She's fine."

"Does she still cry at night?"

"Sometimes."

"Does she still beg to see me? Does she—"

I stopped talking once Emma's blue eyes met mine from the swings. Squealing, she jumped off her seat and ran towards me.

"Daddyyyy! Dadddyyy!" She shouted, but she was picked up before she made it any closer. She was taken away and put inside a car just as she started to cry.

Fuck...

I immediately sat up in bed, realizing that I wasn't in New York City's Central Park. I was in Durham, North Carolina, and I was having another nightmare.

Glancing at the clock on my wall, I saw that it was just past one o'clock. The calendar hanging directly above it only confirmed that I'd been living here for far too long.

All the research I'd done six years ago—weighing the pros and cons, checking the records of all the top firms, and scouring the make-up of women on Date-Match, was now seemingly invalid: The condo I purchased was a mere remnant of what had been advertised, there was only one firm worthy of my time, and the pool of fuck-worthy women was dwindling by the day.

Just hours ago, I'd gone on a date with a woman who told me she was a kindergarten teacher with a penchant for the color red and history books. In reality, she was twice my age, color blind, and she just wanted to "remember what some good cock felt like."

Frustrated, I slipped out of bed and walked down the hallway—straightening the "E" and "H" frames that hung on the wall while trying not to look too hard.

I was going to need more than my usual few shots to get through tonight, and I was starting to become extremely annoyed that I hadn't fucked someone in what felt like forever.

I poured two shots of bourbon and tossed them down back to back. Before I could pour another, my phone vibrated. An email.

Alyssa.

Subject: Performance Quality.

Dear Thoreau,

I'm sure that right now you're in the middle of fucking yet another conquest, and are seconds away from giving her your infamous "One dinner. One night. No repeats." line, but I was just thinking about something and HAD to email you…

If you enjoy sex as much as you claim you do, why do you only insist on one night? Why not a strictly friends with benefits relationship so you won't have so many dry spells? (I mean, this is day thirty of "Operation: Still No Pussy" for you, correct?)

I'm actually starting to wonder if the only reason you give one night is because you already know that your performance won't be good enough to warrant another…

Having a subpar dick isn't the end of the world.

—Alyssa.

I shook my head and typed a response.

Subject: Re: Performance Quality.

Dear Alyssa,

Unfortunately, I am not in the middle of fucking another conquest. Instead I'm busy typing a response to your latest ridiculous email.

This is indeed day thirty of your appropriately named, "Operation: Still No Pussy," but since I've fucked you over the phone and made you cum, it hasn't been a complete failure…

I do in fact enjoy sex—my cock has an insatiable appetite for it, but I've told you countless times that I don't do relationships. Ever.

I refuse to even address your last paragraph, as I've never received a single complaint about my "performance" and my cock is *far* from being subpar.

You are quite correct in your closing statement though: Having a subpar dick really isn't the end of the world.

Having an un-fucked pussy is.

—Thoreau.

My phone rang immediately.

"Seriously?" Alyssa blurted out when I answered. "Does your message really say what I think it says?"

"Have you suddenly forgotten how to read?"

"You are *ridiculous*!" She laughed. "What happened to your date tonight?"

"It was another fucking liar…"

"Aww. Poor Thoreau. I was really hoping the thirtieth day would be the charm."

I rolled my eyes and made another drink. "Is living vicariously through my sex life your newfound hobby?"

"Of course not." Her light laughter drifted over the line, and I could hear the sound of papers shuffling in the background. "I've been meaning to ask you: Where are you from?"

"What do you mean, *where am I from*?"

"Exactly what I asked," she said. "You can't be from the South. There's no drawl or even a hint of an accent in your voice."

I hesitated. "I'm from New York City."

"New York?" Her voice rose an octave. "Why would you ever leave there to come to Durham?"

"It's personal."

"I can't imagine ever wanting to leave New York. It seems so perfect. And there's just something about the lights and the lives of people who stay there, how they all must have these huge dreams and…"

I tuned her out and tossed back my shot. Her poetical waxing about that desolate place needed to be put to a stop. Fast.

"And wouldn't the law firms in New York be far more alluring than the ones here?" She was still talking. "Like, one of my favorite—"

"What's the name of that ballet you're auditioning for this year?" I cut her off.

"*Swan Lake*." She always dropped the subject if I said anything about ballet. "Why?"

"Just wondering. When is the audition?"

"A few months from now. I'm trying as hard as I can to balance my classes—" She cleared her throat. "I mean, I'm trying really hard to balance my case loads with my practice time."

"Why don't you just ask your boss if you can work weekends in exchange for a couple weekdays off?"

"I'm pretty sure that won't work."

"Of course it would work," I said. "There's a lawyer at my firm who works Saturdays through Wednesdays so he can pursue music. If the firm you work for is worth a damn, they'll be flexible with you."

"Yeah, um, I guess I'll have to look into that..."

Silence.

"What firm do you work for?" I asked.

"I can't tell you that."

"What's one of the partners' names?"

"I can't tell you that either."

"But you can tell me how deep you want my cock to be buried inside of you later tonight?"

She sucked in a short breath, a sexy sound that drove me insane the more I heard it.

"How much longer do you think I'm going to put up with just talking to you on the phone, Alyssa?"

"For as long as I want you to." Her voice sounded more confident now.

"You think I'm going to talk to you for another month without being able to fuck you? Without being able to see you in person?"

"I think you'll talk to me for several months without fucking me. As a matter of fact, I think you'll talk to me for *years* without fucking me because I'm your friend, and friends—"

"If I haven't fucked you within the next month or two, we won't be *friends* anymore."

"You want to bet?"

"I don't have to." I hung up and grabbed my laptop, ready to give Date-Match another try. The second I clicked the prettiest woman on the page, an email from Alyssa popped onto my screen.

Subject: Trust Me.
You and I will still be friends a few months from now, and you'll be completely okay with not seeing my face.

Watch.

—Alyssa.

Subject: Re: Trust Me.
You and I will be *fucking* a few months from now, and the only reason I'll be okay with not seeing your face is because you'll be riding my cock as I bend your ass over a table.

Watch.

—Thoreau.

testimony (n.):

Oral evidence given under oath by a witness in answer to questions posed by attorneys at trial or at a deposition.

Andrew

"Miss Everhart, you can take the floor and question Mr. Hamilton now," Mr. Greenwood said from across the courtroom.

It was the last day of the month, which meant that we were finally getting use out of the million dollar courtroom that sat on the top floor of GBH. There was no need for this room, but since the firm had more money than it knew what to do with, the space was being used for the interns' mock cases.

Today's "trial" was about some idiot who defrauded his own company's employees—leaving them without insurance and health care, and unfortunately, I was playing the accused.

Standing up from the defense table, Aubrey grabbed her notebook and took the floor. She and I hadn't spoken since I kicked her out of my condo two weeks ago, but from what I could tell, she seemed unfazed.

She'd been smiling quite often, being extremely nice, and each time she delivered my coffee she did it with a smirk and an, "I really hope you enjoy this coffee, *Mr. Hamilton*."

I'd been stopping at the coffee shop up the street ever since…

"Mr. Hamilton," she said, smoothing her tight blue dress, "is it true that you previously cheated on your wife?"

"I've *never* cheated."

"Stick to the character, Andrew." Mr. Bach whispered from the judge's seat.

I rolled my eyes. "Yes. There was a time when I cheated on my wife."

"Why?"

"Objection!" One of the interns shouted. "Your Honor, do we really need to know the specifics about my client's love life? This mock trial is about his involvement in a conspiracy."

"If I may, Your Honor," Aubrey spoke before the "judge" could say anything. "I think assessing how Mr. Hamilton behaved in his previous affairs is a good assessment of his character. If we were trying a client who abandoned his company due to incompetence, it wouldn't be out of line for me to ask about his previous personal relationships—especially if our mock client is a high profile one."

"Overruled."

Aubrey smiled and looked at her notebook. "Do you have commitment problems, Mr. Hamilton?"

"How can I have a problem with something I don't believe in?"

"So, you believe in engaging in one night stands for the rest of your life?"

"*Your Honor...*" The opposing intern stood up, but I raised my hand.

"No need," I said, narrowing my eyes at Aubrey. "I'll entertain Miss Everhart's inappropriate line of questioning...I believe in living my life however the hell I want and dealing with women whenever I want to deal with them. I'm not sure how who I sleep with has anything to do with this mock conspiracy case, but since we're discussing my sex life, you should know that I'm happy and satisfied. I have a date later tonight actually. Would you like me to report the details to you and the jury tomorrow?"

The interns in the jury box laughed as Aubrey's smile faded. Even as she forced it again, I could see a hint of hurt in her eyes.

"So…" She took a deep breath. "Regarding the case—"

"So happy you're finally getting on topic."

The jurors laughed again.

"Do you believe in morals, Mr. Hamilton?" she asked.

"Yes."

"Do you think you possess them?"

"I think everyone does to a certain extent."

"Permission to approach the witness?" She looked at Mr. Bach and he nodded.

"Mr. Hamilton, can you read the highlighted portion of this document please?" She placed a sheet of paper in front of me, and I noticed a small handwritten note at the very top of the page: *"I fucking hate you and I wish I'd never met you."*

"Yes," I said, taking a pen out of my pocket. "It says that my company was unaware of insurance policy changes at the time."

As she handed a copy of the document to the jury panel, I wrote a response to her note: *"Sorry to see that you regret meeting me, as I don't regret meeting you—only that I fucked you more than once."*

She asked me to read another section to the court, and then she took the paper away—glaring at me once she read my words.

I tried to look away from her, to focus on something else, but the way she looked today prevented that from happening. Her hair wasn't up in her signature bun—it was falling past her shoulders in long curls that grazed her breasts. And the dress she was wearing, a highly inappropriate one that hugged her thighs a little too tightly, rose up an inch every time she took a step.

"I have three more questions for Mr. Hamilton, Your Honor," she said.

"There's no limit, Miss Everhart." He smiled.

"Right…" She stepped forward and looked into my eyes. "Mr. Hamilton, you and your company led your employees to believe that you cared about them, that you had their best interests at heart, and that you would literally communicate the actual changes you would make before termination. Are those promises not directly from your company's brochure?"

"They are."

"So, do you believe that you deserve to be fined or punished for giving your employees false hope? For dragging them into a situation you knew you would end all along?"

"I think I did what was in my *company's* best interest," I said—ignoring the fact that my heart was pounding against my chest. "And in the future, as those *employees* move on like they should, they'll perhaps realize that my company wasn't the best fit for them anyway."

"Don't you think you owe them a simple apology? Don't you think you should at least give them that?"

"An apology implies that I did something *wrong*." I gritted my teeth. "Just because they don't agree with what I did, doesn't mean that I wasn't right."

"Do you believe in reasonable doubt, Mr. Hamilton?"

"You said you only had three questions left. Has elementary mathematics changed recently?"

"Do you believe in reasonable doubt, *Mr. Hamilton*?" Her face reddened. "Yes or no?"

"*Yes*." I clenched my jaw. "Yes, I believe that's a common requirement for every single lawyer in this country."

"So, given the current case that we're discussing…Do you think that someone like you, someone who treated his employees so terribly, could ever change in the future, now that you know how badly you've hurt others' livelihood?"

"Reasonable doubt is not about *feelings*, Miss Everhart, and I suggest you consult the closest legal dictionary you can find because I'm pretty sure we've had this discussion once before…"

"I don't recall that, Mr. Hamilton, but—"

"In your own ill-fated yet correct words, didn't you once tell me—post your first interview here at GBH, that certain lies have to be told and certain truths have to be withheld? And that the ultimate conviction is up to those who can discern which is which?" I looked her up and down. "Is that not the exact definition that you provided for reasonable doubt?"

She stared at me a long time—giving me that same look of hurt she had when I kicked her out of my place.

"No further questions, Your Honor." She mumbled.

Mr. Greenwood clapped loudly from the back of the room. Mr. Bach and the other interns followed suit.

"Very good job, Miss Everhart!" Mr. Bach shouted. "That was a very direct yet compelling line of questioning."

"Thank you sir." She avoided looking at me.

"You are officially the first intern to get our Andrew all riled up." He smiled, seemingly impressed. "We definitely need to keep you around. Hell, we may call you in when we need to be reminded that he's capable of showing emotion."

More laughter.

"Great job today, everyone!" He leaned back in the judge's chair. "We'll go over your presentations later this week and email you the scores next Thursday." He banged his gavel. "Court adjourned."

The interns filed out of the room and Aubrey looked over her shoulder one last time, shooting me an angry look.

I shot one right back, grateful that I had a date tonight so I could fuck her and her stupid questions out of my mind.

Seven o'clock can't get here soon enough…

I waited a few minutes before heading to the elevator and attempted to remember my schedule for the rest of the day. I had two consultations with small business owners this afternoon, and I needed to make a Starbucks run before Aubrey could bring me my next cup of coffee.

I unlocked the door to my office and hit the lights, prepared to call for Jessica, but Ava was standing in front of my bookshelf.

"Is the homeless shelter not open today?" I asked.

"I came here to finally give you what you asked for."

"It's a little too early to jump off a bridge."

"I'm being serious."

"As am I." I walked past her and sent a quick text on my phone. "If you jump before noon, the news crew won't be able to run the story during primetime."

She stepped in front of my desk and set down a manila folder. "I won't drag your name through the courts anymore, I won't file anymore stays or injunctions, and I won't make any false claims about your character either…I'm done lying now."

"I'm sure." I picked up the papers. "In other words, there's a new guy you're anxious to fuck over. Does he know the real you?"

"Seriously? You're getting your precious divorce. Why do you even care?"

"I don't." I put on my reading glasses and looked over the documents. "No alimony requests, abuse claims, or demands for property? Am I missing a page?"

"I'm telling you. I'm done lying."

I didn't believe her for one second, but I picked up my phone and called the notary, telling her it was an emergency.

"You know…" Ava leaned against my desk. "I remember the cake you bought me for our wedding anniversary. It was white and light blue, and it had all these pretty little NYC decorations on it. It had flavored layers, too. One for every year that we were together. Do you remember that?"

"I remember you fucking my best friend."

"We can't have one nice moment before we end things for good?"

"You and I ended a long time ago, Ava." I tried to keep my voice flat, monotonous. "When something is over, the final words—good or bad, don't make much of a fucking difference."

She sighed and I noticed how terrible she looked today. Her eyes were bloodshot, her hair was frizzy and tied into a loose ponytail, and even though the blue dress she was wearing fit perfectly, she hadn't made an attempt to iron it.

"What's this so called emergency you have, Mr. Hamilton?" The notary walked into the room, smiling. "Are you requesting that we purchase another thousand dollar coffee maker?" She stopped talking once she saw Ava.

"Miss Kannan, this is Ava Sanchez, my soon to be ex-wife. I need you to witness the signing of the divorce papers and make three copies—sealing one of them for mailing purposes."

She nodded and pulled a stamper out of her pocket.

"Did you notice that I willingly gave up our condo on the West End to you?" Ava asked.

"The condo that *I* bought?" I signed my name. "How generous."

"We made a lot of memories in that house."

"Signing papers doesn't require conversation," I said.

She snatched the pen away from me and placed her signature above mine—taking extra time to add a double swirl to the last letter.

"I'll be right back with your copies." Miss Kannan avoided looking at either of us as she shuffled out of the room.

"So, that's it, I guess," Ava said. "I'm officially out of your life."

"No." I shook my head. "Unfortunately, you're still in my sight."

"Would it kill you to wish me the best? To at least tell me good luck?"

"Seeing as though you're going back to prison, I guess that would be appropriate." I shrugged. "Good luck. The authorities are outside waiting for you, so take all the time you need. There's even a vending machine down the hall if you want to taste freedom one last time…Although, since you'll be locked up with plenty of women, I'm sure eating pussy after the lights go out will taste just as good."

"You fucking snitched on me?" Her face went white as I held up my phone, showing her the text I sent the second I saw her in my office. "How could you do that to me?"

"How could I *not*?"

"Did I really hurt you that badly, Liam? Did I—"

"Don't you ever fucking call me that."

"Did I hurt you that badly?" She repeated, shaking her head.

I didn't answer.

"This is…This is about *Emma* isn't it?" She hissed. "Is that what this is? You're still holding that shit over my head?"

"Get the fuck out. *Now*."

"It's been six years, Liam. Six. Fucking. Years. You need to let that go." She opened the door and a sly smile spread across her face. "Things like that happen all the time…As unfortunate as it was, it helped make you the man you are today, didn't it?"

It took everything in me to stay seated, to not lunge after her.

Seething, I waited for her to leave and walked over to my window—watching as she stepped into the parking lot, as she raised her hands in the air as the officers shouted at her.

Then, just like six years ago, she smiled through the handcuffing process, and laughed when they tossed her into the back of the car.

The black fleet slowly drove away, and a familiar pang hit my chest.

Grabbing my keys, I rushed to the parking lot and slipped into my car—subconsciously telling myself to go home, consciously driving toward the nearest beach.

I put my phone on silent as I hit the highway, and as the seconds dissolved into hours, the city disappeared in the rearview mirror. The buildings appeared farther and farther apart, and eventually the only thing outside my window were trees and sand.

When I finally reached a secluded bay, I parked my car in front of a rock. I opened my glove compartment and took out the red folder Aubrey once tried to open. Then I stepped out and sat on the closest bench.

Taking a deep breath, I pulled out the photos and promised myself that this would be the last time I looked at them: Me and my daughter walking along the shore of New Jersey's beach as the sun set. Her smiling as I picked up a seashell and held it against her ear. Me carrying her on my shoulders and pointing to a starry night sky.

Even though I knew doing this would lead to cold sweats and an inevitable nightmare later, I continued flipping through the photos.

Even the ones without me: The ones of her looking sad and lonely at the park, the ones of her looking off into the distance for something—or *someone*, that wasn't there.

Emma…

My heart clenched at the final frame in the set. It was a shot of her fiddling with her umbrella, crying. She was upset because they were forcing her to go inside, because they didn't understand that although she liked being at the park in broad sunlight, she preferred to play outside in the rain.

emotional distress (n.):

A negative emotional reaction—which may include fear, anger, anxiety, and suffering for which monetary damages may be awarded.

Aubrey

I looked terrible. Absolutely terrible.

Today was the first full costume rehearsal for *Swan Lake* and I didn't look fit for the part at all. My eyes were swollen and puffy—ruined from randomly crying about Andrew, my lips were dry and cracked, and my skin was so pale that Mr. Petrova walked by and asked, "Are you playing a white swan or are you playing a *white ghost*?"

As much as I tried to force myself to smile through my heartache, I was crying every moment I was alone, eating an exorbitant amount of ice cream and chocolate each night, and I couldn't sleep for shit.

I still couldn't believe Andrew kicked me out of his condo so cruelly. One minute he was holding me against his chest and kissing me, and the next he was telling me that he and I had fucked enough—that he didn't want me anymore, and that he was going to fuck someone else.

What was worse, was that when we returned to work that following Monday, he'd been twice as rude to me. He reassigned me to a case that would take me months to sort, scolded me in front of everyone for being ten seconds late, and then he had the audacity to complain about me smiling as I brought him his daily coffee.

At least I spit in it...

"Are you crying right now?" The make-up assistant tilted my chin up. "Do you know how expensive this stage mascara is?"

"I'm sorry." I froze my eyeballs to their sockets and held back tears.

"I didn't see your parents' names on the guest list for today. Are they coming to the second run through on Saturday?"

"No."

"I guess they just want to see the full on show with no stops then, huh?" She laughed. "My parents are the same way. I told them about the number of run-throughs we have to do and they said they'll see it when it's finished. They're all about perfection."

"Unfortunately, I can relate..."

She laughed and blabbered on and on, making me silently count the seconds until she was done.

When she pressed my face with the last puff of powder, she spun me around to face the mirror on the other side of the room.

"Wow..." I whispered. "Seriously, wow..."

I didn't look like I'd been crying at all. Although my eyelids were covered in dark eye shadow, and she'd dabbed a fake tear trail past my right eye, I looked as if I was the happiest woman on earth.

"Miss Everhart?" Mr. Petrova asked, stepping behind me. "May I borrow you for a second?"

"Yes, sir." I followed him through the backstage doors and outside to the empty stretching area.

"Have a seat on the bench, Miss Everhart." He took a cigarette out of his pocket and lit it.

The smoke unfurled in spirals between us and he looked me up and down. For some odd reason, he looked more upset than usual, like he was about to yell at me.

"Mr. Petrova..." I said softly. "Did I do something wrong?"

"No." He shook his head. "I brought you out here alone because I want you to know that you looked fat during practice yesterday. *Too fat*."

"What?"

"Even though you danced the part of the black swan beautifully, capturing the right degree of anger and sadness, you failed—*fucking failed*, with the white swan." He coughed. "You looked like your mind was elsewhere. Like it was killing you to be happy for five minutes, and to top it off, you've gotten fat."

I rolled my eyes and tuned him out, focusing on the cars whirring down the street. I wasn't disturbed by his insults anymore. Him calling me fat was nothing compared to the things he said to me last week.

"*Miss Everhart*?" His voice snapped me out of my thoughts.

"Yes?"

"I need you to open that later," he said, patting me on my shoulder. "It's very important."

"Open what?"

"Do you not see the envelope I just placed on your lap?" He put out his cigarette. "Do I need to tell your understudy that she needs to get ready to dance?"

"No." I picked up the envelope, running my fingers along the crease. "You don't need to do that, sir."

"Good." He walked toward the building and held the door open. "Now, make me believe that I picked the right girl to be my swan."

"The Walters will be over for dinner next Sunday at six and we need you to make an appearance," my mother said to me over the phone that night. "I think they're going to write us a very nice check for the campaign."

"How exciting."

"It is exciting, isn't it?" She practically squealed. "Everything is happening so fast and falling into place quite perfectly. We're gathering funding, planning the advertising, and..."

I set my phone on the table and made myself a bucket of ice water, wincing with every step I took. I was sure that I would have a new set of blisters at the end of this week, but after the way I danced at today's run-through, they would be well-worth it.

I completed every jump with ease, matched my peers step for step, and at the end—when the final number called for ten pirouettes, I did fifteen. Everyone in the audience gave me a standing ovation, but Mr. Petrova sat silently rubbing his chin.

He stared at me, tilted his head to the side, and simply said, "Today's practice is over." That was the biggest compliment he'd ever given.

Smiling at the memory, I carried the ice bucket over to the couch and set it down. I slipped my feet inside and held the phone up to my ear again.

"Oh, and the Yarboroughs..." My mother was still talking. "They're considering throwing a small benefit in your father's honor next month at the country club. You'll need to be present for that and it won't be casual, so I'd really prefer if you wore your hair in curls please. There will be a photographer from the local paper there."

"Are you going to ask how my day went?"

"In a minute. Did you receive the dress I sent yesterday?"

I looked at the plastic bag draped over my door. "There was a rough run through of *Swan Lake* today. It was for the costume designers, to see if everything looked right under the new lights. It was the best run through we've had so far."

"Have you tried on that dress yet? Do you think you'll be able to do it tonight?"

"Mom..."

"I need to have it tailored for Sunday's dinner ASAP if it doesn't fit."

"Could you just say, I honestly don't give a fuck about your life, Aubrey?" I groaned as my toes finally felt the effect of the ice. "That would make me feel ten times better right now."

"*Aubrey Nicole Everhart…*" She enunciated every syllable of my name. "Have you lost your mind?"

"No, but I'm starting to lose my tolerance for talking to you on the phone. Why bother calling if you only want to hear yourself talk?"

She didn't get a chance to answer.

There was a call on my other line, so I clicked over without mentioning it.

"Hello?" I answered.

"Is this Aubrey Everhart?" It was a male's voice.

"Yes. This is she."

"Great! This is Greg Houston. I'm the student enrollment chair, and I was just calling to let you know that your withdrawal from the university has been approved! It'll be official once you come in and personally sign off on the forms. I personally think it's great that you're taking time off to help out with your father's campaign."

"*WHAT*?!"

"That's a very selfless thing of you to do, Miss Everhart," he said. "I'm sure whenever you decide to come back, the academic committee will offer you credit for your real world experience. Anyway, I noticed you filled out the electronic forms, but since you live within a fifty mile radius of the school, its policy that you have to sign them manually as well. Also, regarding the credits you've earned at the university thus far…"

Everything around me went black.

I couldn't believe this shit.

I wanted to click over and shout at my mother, to ask how dare she and my father pull me out of college without even telling me, but I couldn't. I simply hung up and sat still—stone-faced and lost.

There were tears falling down my face, but I couldn't feel them. I couldn't feel a damn thing.

I pressed the power button on my phone to prevent anyone else from calling me and pulled out the envelope Mr. Petrova gave me earlier. I assumed it was a long list of insults, or a new diet, but it was a letter:

Miss Everhart,

I just received notice that you were leaving the university at the end of this term. While I am disappointed in your failure to alert me to this news in advance, I am impressed with the growth you have shown while being in my program.

You are still an average dancer, but considering the fact that your peers are all terrible dancers, I guess you can be somewhat proud of that status.

Behind this letter is a recommendation for the New York City Ballet Company. Due to a few unfortunate circumstances, several spots have opened for their current class. This does not happen often, and you would be quite stupid not to audition.

However, if you do audition and are not accepted, it will only mean that you didn't dance your best. (Or that you gained another unfortunate pound.)
—Petrova.

I flipped to the attached page and noticed that the deadline to audition was in three weeks, that if I auditioned and was accepted, I would be leaving my current leading role behind and would have to start all over again.

Dancing for the NYC Ballet Company had once been a dream of mine, but after I broke my foot at sixteen, I readjusted my version of a dream career; the competition at such a place would be far too fierce for someone who sat out a complete year, full recovery or not.

Nonetheless, I couldn't fathom going away to New York City, not alone anyway. And I didn't think I could leave Andrew without at least getting a much deserved apology.

Sighing, I turned on my laptop and logged into my email, shocked to see his name at the very top of my inbox.

Subject: Mock Trials.

Miss Everhart,

For the third time this week, you've alluded to our former affairs in the court room. Although I am not surprised by this, I am quite disappointed.

You may regret the aftermath of fucking me, but I know damn well that you loved every single second that my cock was inside of you. (And before you lie and say that you didn't, think about the numerous times you screamed my name as my mouth devoured your pussy.)

Maybe if you thought about those things instead of your uncontrollable and erratic "feelings," your defenses in court wouldn't be so laughable.

—Andrew

I deleted his email and read Petrova's letter again.

I needed to research the New York City Ballet auditions *tonight.*

malfeasance (n.):

Intentionally doing something either legally or morally wrong which one had no right to do.

Andrew

I opened my left drawer, searching for a bottle of aspirin. I hadn't slept well in over a week, and I was certain that most of that had to do with the half-assed reports the interns were giving me. That, or Aubrey was poisoning my lunch.

I flipped through her most recent report and groaned as I read her handwritten remarks: *"I find it very ironic that you can give us an assignment on the importance of trust and relationships, when you have no idea what either of those words mean. PS—You did not "devour" my pussy."*

I tore off her note and tossed it into the trash, reading the next one: *"A case that deals with a boss fucking his employee? At least this boss had the balls to come clean and admit that he actually liked her, instead of tossing her away like trash. PS—Yesterday's extra ingredient in your coffee was flakes of melted super glue. I hope you enjoyed it."*

"Mr. Hamilton?" Jessica stepped into my office.

"Yes?"

"Would you like me to send your Armani suit to another dry cleaning company?" she asked. "This is the third time you've sent them those pants. I don't think that brown stain is coming out."

"No, thank you." I sighed. "Just order me some new ones please."

"Will do!" She batted her eyes at me as she left, and I immediately emailed Aubrey.

Subject: Super Glue.

I no longer drink your fucking coffee, but since you've once again proven how much of a novice you are when it comes to the law, I'll be saving your handwritten note so my friends will know who to charge with my murder.

Grow up.

—Andrew

Subject: Re: Super Glue.

You don't have any friends. I was your only one. And I don't care if you save my handwritten note because I've saved all of your EMAILS—especially the ones that say, "Come to my office so I can eat your pussy on my lunch break," or "I love the way your mouth looks when you wrap it around my cock."

You first.

—Aubrey.

I started typing my response—not willing to give her the last word, but I heard Jessica clearing her throat.

"Something else I can help you with today?" I looked up. "I could've sworn you just left my office."

"Word around the firm is that today is your birthday."

"Today is *not* my birthday."

"That's not what HR said."

"HR is full of shit." I looked at the coffee mug on the edge of my desk, noticing that the coffee wasn't even brown. It was orange. "But speaking of HR, could you have them ban Miss Everhart from touching the coffee machines?"

"Doubt it." She stepped closer. "Between you and me, we're throwing you a surprise party in the break room. Like, right now. We've been waiting for you to take a break but you haven't, so… Can you step in for a second?"

"Did you just tell me no about my coffee machine request?"

"I'll handle it after you come to your party." She smiled and reached for my hand, but I stood on my own.

"I've told your grandfather on multiple occasions that I don't appreciate his employee birthday parties."

She shrugged and led me down the hall. "Make sure you look surprised. I put a lot of work into this…I always go the extra mile for you."

I ignored the way she was licking her lips.

She pushed the door open, and all of the staff tossed confetti into the air and shouted, "Happy Birthday, Mr. Hamilton!" Then they began to sing the birthday song—out of tune and terribly off key.

I walked over to the windows where they'd placed a small white cake with blue candles, and blew them out before the song ended.

"Happy Birthday, Andrew!" Mr. Greenwood handed me a blue envelope. "How old are you today?"

"Seeing as though today is not my birthday, I'm the same age as I was yesterday."

He laughed, still incapable of catching when I was being short with him. Holding his stomach in jest, he motioned for one of the interns to take our photo.

As the camera flashed, I spotted Aubrey standing in a corner with her arms crossed. She was shaking her head at everyone, and when her eyes finally met mine, she scowled.

"I got you something…" Jessica pressed a small black box into my hand. "But I think you need to open it behind closed doors, when you're alone and thinking about me." She blushed and walked away.

I made a mental note to toss whatever it was into the trash. And instead of immediately leaving the party, I walked around the room and said thank you to everyone—reminding each intern that "birthday" or not, the assignments were still due at the end of the day.

I approached Aubrey with my hand outstretched, but she recoiled and walked into the adjoining ante-room.

"Are you seriously this immature, Miss Everhart?" I followed her, spinning her around to face me as the door shut.

"Are you seriously this cruel?" She glared at me. "You gave me more work than anyone else this morning just so you could berate me in front of them later, just because you think I embarrassed you in court again."

"You'd actually have to know what the fuck you were doing if you wanted to embarrass me in court." I unintentionally grabbed her hands, rubbing my fingers against her skin. "And I gave you more work so you wouldn't have time to make my coffee, which up until this morning, I only *assumed* you were poisoning."

"Since when is 'spit' poison?"

"You owe me another fucking suit…" I lowered my voice. "Do you have any idea how much—"

"*No.*" She cut me off. "Do you have any idea how much you've changed? I actually miss when I was Alyssa and you were Thoreau."

"Back when you were a *fucking liar*?"

"Back when you treated me better…" She stared into my eyes—giving a look of longing, and my hands went around her waist, pulling her against me.

My mouth was on hers in seconds and we were kissing like we hadn't seen each other in years—fighting each other for control. I trailed my fingers against the zipper at the back of her dress, feeling my cock hardening against her thigh.

She pressed herself against my chest and let me slip my tongue deeper into her mouth, but she eventually tore away and pushed me.

Looking absolutely disgusted, she turned away and stormed out of the room.

I straightened my tie before following her into the party room, but she was no longer there.

"Are you going to cut the cake, Andrew?" Mr. Bach called out. "Or do you want Jessica to do it for another year in a row?"

Jessica held up the knife and winked at me.

"Jessica can cut it," I said. "I'll be right back." I stepped out and headed for the interns' offices—walking straight toward Aubrey's cubicle.

Her face was beet red and she was stuffing folders into her bag.

"I didn't give you permission to leave early." I stepped in front of her.

"I didn't give you permission to treat me like shit, but you've done one hell of a job, haven't you?"

"You just said that I wasn't treating you like shit when I thought your name was *Alyssa*, when I thought you were a fucking lawyer."

"That makes your current treatment of me acceptable?"

"It makes it *justifiable*."

Silence.

"I can't do this anymore, Andrew…" She shook her head.

"Does that mean you'll stop acting like a child in court? Does it mean—"

"Here." She cut me off and pressed a silver box against my chest. "I bought this for you a few weeks ago, back when Jessica was planning your birthday party."

"Did you spit in it?"

"I should have." She picked up her bag and rushed past me, heading for the exit.

A part of me actually wanted to go after her and make her explain what the hell she meant about "not doing this anymore," but I knew doing so would be pointless. Talking to her for less than three minutes aroused me, and I needed to remember why I ended "us" in the first place.

I returned to the break-room and said thank you to the last of the interns, glancing at the photo HR had pinned on the wall. It was a collage of my professional photos with a birthday hat sticker attached to my head. And they'd written "Happy Birthday, Andrew! GBH Loves You!" in bright blue.

In all actuality, my birthday was months from now—in December, a day I hadn't celebrated in a very long time. And even though I'd never publicly admit it, I somewhat liked the fact that the people at GBH were willing to celebrate my birthday—real or not.

"How many slices of cake would you like me to wrap up for you, Mr. Hamilton?" Jessica tapped my shoulder.

"Three," I said. "And I'll take a cup of lemonade, too."

"You're not going to stay for the "Who Knows Mr. Hamilton the Best" game?"

"None of you know me." I returned to my office and locked the door, setting the new birthday gifts on top of my bookshelf.

The envelope from Mr. Greenwood contained a note that said he appreciated my hard work and dedication to the firm. Beneath his written words was a gift card to his family's other multimillion dollar entity: A golf course.

The gifts from the interns were all "I.O.U." letters that begged for extra time on their assignments. I held all of those over my shredder.

Jessica's black box was next, and as much as I wanted to throw it away and never think of it again, I couldn't resist knowing what she bought me. I took the top off and removed the paper, pulling out a soft piece of silk and a note:

"I overheard that you like to keep these in your pocket…Here are mine. PS—I took them off in the bathroom five minutes ago :-)"

Jesus…

I buried her panties at the bottom of my trashcan and crumpled that note.

I stared at Aubrey's silver box for a while, wondering if I should wait until later to unwrap it, but I couldn't help peeling off the paper.

Inside of the box was a small black photo frame. It was handcrafted—bordered with iron pressed images of pointe slippers, law scales, and the words "Alyssa" and "Thoreau" in smooth white letters.

The picture in it was one of us, one of her laying against my chest in my bed and smiling at the camera. Her cheeks were flushed red—like they always were after sex, and she was dressed in one of my T-shirts.

I remembered her forcing me to take that photo—insisting that she "wouldn't share it with anyone" and only wanted it for herself. She even forced me to smile…

I set the frame down and took out the other object in the box—a sparkling silver watch with an inscription etched across its back:

Subject: You.
I liked you as "Thoreau," but I love you as Andrew.
—Aubrey (Alyssa)

My glass of wine sat untouched at Arbors Restaurant, and the candles in the centerpiece were shedding sheets of their wax onto the table.

I was expecting a date any moment now, but I couldn't stop staring at the watch Aubrey gave me. She'd clearly thought about each and every part of the design; no element was by mistake.

I noticed two interlocking A's in the corner of its screen, and earlier, in the sunlight, I'd noticed that my name was etched on the edge of its frame.

"Are you Thoreau?" A woman's voice interrupted my thoughts, making me look up.

"I am."

She smiled and took the seat across from me. "I hope you don't mind, but I'm a regular here and the waitress asked if I'd be having my usual when I arrived. I told her you would have the same."

"I don't mind at all." A small feeling of guilt welled inside my chest, but it wasn't enough to distract me from pursuing what I needed tonight: Pussy. ASAP.

The waitress placed two steamed dishes in front of us, and I checked the time. I was only giving this woman one hour.

"So, what type of cases do you normally handle?" she asked.

"Corporate for the most part, but I've done government and tax as well."

"Interesting. Have you lived in Durham long?"

"Too long."

"And is this your normal M.O.?" She leaned back in her chair, dragging her nails against her see-through top. "One night stands?"

"Is that a problem for you?"

"It never is."

I raised my eyebrow and looked her over. She was actually quite appealing—long blond hair, curvy figure, and perky breasts.

Physical attributes aside, we seemed to have a lot in common. She was a real lawyer in the next county over, she read most of the same books, and from what she'd told me over the phone, we shared a comparable sexual appetite.

Our entrees came and went, the conversation plodded along, but Aubrey's watch still had a part of my attention.

"Is something bothering you?" My date waved her hand in front of my face. "I remember you being a lot more talkative over the phone."

"I'm fine." I waved the waiter over for the check. "Just tired."

"Too tired to fuck?"

"I'm *never* too tired to fuck."

Blushing, she crossed her legs and leaned over the table. "I've been looking forward to this all week."

I didn't respond. I simply signed the check and stood up, holding out my hand for her.

We walked through the hotel lobby and straight for the elevators.

The second the doors closed, she pressed her lips against mine and threaded her fingers through my hair.

"Fuck…" I groaned as one of her hands slid down to my belt.

She moved her mouth down my neck as we ascended to the top floor, grazing her teeth against my skin. Moaning, she gasped as I gripped her waist and kissed her back—controlling her tongue with mine.

I pulled the band away from her ponytail and tossed it to the floor. I closed my eyes and deepened our kiss—torturously biting her lip as she tried to pull away.

Sliding her knee between my legs, she unfastened my belt and tugged at my zipper. "How long are we going to fuck tonight?"

"As long as you want." I palmed her breasts through her shirt, slipping a hand underneath her bra.

"*Ahhhh…*" She murmured as I caressed her nipple.

The elevator doors slid open quickly, but our bodies remained entwined as we found our way to the suite. Her lips latched onto mine again as we stumbled into the room—bumping into the lamps and the dressers.

She was moaning louder now, barely controlling herself as I unzipped her dress and unclasped her bra.

I felt her hands at my waist—pushing my pants to the floor, and when my back hit the wall, I realized she was on her knees in front of me.

Leaning forward, she rubbed her hands up and down my cock, asking me to tell her how badly I wanted her mouth on me.

"I don't…" I shook my head as I realized I had been fantasizing about Aubrey the entire time.

"You're not even going to beg for it?" She smiled, bringing her head closer.

"Stop." I grabbed her by her hair and gently pushed her away.

"Is something wrong, Thoreau? Did you want to do me first instead? Should I get on the bed or the chair?"

I couldn't make out the rest of her questions; images of Aubrey were clouding my brain, invading all my senses. And the more I stared at this woman, a woman who was nowhere near as beautiful as Aubrey, the more I felt my cock softening.

Fuck…

I pulled my pants up and zipped the fly. "I no longer feel like fucking you. You can leave."

"*Excuse me*?" She sucked in a breath and crossed her arms. "What did you just say?"

"I said that I don't feel like fucking you." I spoke slowly. "And that you can leave. Enjoy the rest of your night."

"You're going to put me out? Just like that?"

"Would you like me to reserve another room for you?"

"What happened to the man I met online?" She stood up. "Was that all a front? Is this some type of game where you take out women, say sexy things you've probably read off the internet, and then make them get naked knowing damn well that you don't know how to fuck?"

"I definitely know how to fuck." I narrowed my eyes at her. "I just don't feel like fucking *you*."

"I can't…I can't believe…" Her jaw dropped. "You're a fucking asshole!"

"Asshole? Yes. Fucking? Unfortunately not. Can you make sure that the door is completely closed on your way out?"

She pulled her dress over her body and picked up her purse. "I'm putting a flag next to your profile on Date-Match. And you know what else? I'm going to leave a review of our encounter, too. I'm going to make sure—"

"Do you normally talk as you get dressed?" I cut her off and took a seat on the bed. "I'm pretty sure it's something that doesn't require conversation."

Fuming, she slipped into her shoes and rushed out of the room—slamming the door behind her.

I waited until I heard the ping of the elevator and lay across the mattress. I tried my best to think of something or someone other than Aubrey, but she was all that came to mind.

What the fuck is happening?

I stared at the ceiling for another hour, unable to take my mind off of how her mouth felt against mine at the office earlier today. Even if it was only for a few seconds.

Needing to get to the bottom of this, I pulled my phone out of my pocket and called her.

"Hello?" She answered on the second ring. "Hello?"

"Why did you buy me that watch, Aubrey?"

"Why do you care?"

"I don't, but I read the inscription on the back."

Silence.

"I need to ask you something," I said.

"Only if I can ask you a few things first…"

"Go ahead."

"How can you possibly be so adamant about honesty when you haven't been completely honest with me?"

"I *have* been completely honest with you."

"I'm starting to believe that your name isn't really Andrew Hamilton..."

"So you're still stalking me and my past online? Do you not have any other hobbies?"

"Who is *EH*?" Her voice cracked. "Why are those two letters hanging on all your walls? Why are they engraved in all of your cufflinks?"

"*Aubrey...*"

"What's going on with you and Ava? I saw her walk out of your office last week, and she smirked at me."

"Is this a bad time to talk?"

"*Yes.*" She was breathing hard. "This is a very bad time. Why don't you just hang up and go to the Marriott so you can fuck someone else?"

"I *am* at the Marriott, and I was actually about to fuck some-one else."

She was silent for several seconds. "I don't...I don't want to hear from you anymore, Andrew."

"What did you just say?"

"I said I don't want to hear from you anymore. Don't you ever fucking call me again." She hung up.

impasse (n.):

The inability of two parties to reach a negotiated settlement.

A few days later…

Aubrey

My heart was still aching—reeling, and although I'd told Andrew never to call me again, and that I didn't want to hear from him, I couldn't move on until I received an apology.

I *needed* it…

I felt sick to my stomach after giving him that watch, and I'd foolishly expected for him to call and say, "I love you, too," but he acted as if it meant nothing.

Without knocking, I opened the door to his office and shut it behind me.

He raised his eyebrow as I stepped over to his desk, but he didn't hang up his phone.

"Yes, that will be fine," he spoke into the receiver.

"I need to talk to you." I blurted out. "*Now.*"

He motioned for me to take a seat, but he continued talking. "Yes. That will work as well."

I sat and crossed my arms, trying not to stare at him too hard. He was utter perfection today—looking more fuck-able than usual with a fresh hair-cut and a brand new grey suit. His eyes regarded me intensely as usual, and I noticed he was actually wearing the watch I gave him. He'd even paired it with matching cufflinks.

Maybe I'm overreacting after all…

"Right…" He leaned back in his chair and typed a few things onto his keyboard. "I'll see you at eight o'clock tonight, Sandra. Room 225."

My stomach dropped.

"Something I can help you with, Miss Everhart?" He hung up the phone. "Is there any reason why you barged into my office without knocking?"

"You've fucked someone else already?"

"Is that a serious question?"

"Did you fuck someone else already? Did you?"

"Would it matter?"

"Yes, it would fucking matter…" My blood boiled as I stood up. "*Did you sleep with someone else*?"

"Not yet." He narrowed his eyes at me and stood up too, walking over to me. "However, I really don't see how that's any of your concern."

I looked at his wrist. "Why are you wearing that watch if you don't feel the same way I do?"

"It's the only watch that matches my new cufflinks."

"Are you seriously this blind?" There were tears welling in my eyes. "Are you—"

"I told you a long time ago that I don't do feelings—that if we ever did fuck, that would be the end of us." He tucked a strand of hair behind my ear. "However, I do realize that by crossing the line with you, personally and professionally, that a percentage of the blame is mine."

"A *percentage*?"

"Would you like me to bring in the firm's accountant? I'm sure he can work out the exact figure."

"Andrew…" I was on the verge of losing it.

"Since we did break the boundaries, and we were in fact friends before, I'm willing to revert to that arrangement."

I shook my head as he tilted my chin up and looked into my eyes.

"We can still talk on the phone at night," he said. "You can tell me about your ballet, your parents, your life…And, to be sensitive to your feelings, I'll tell you about my life but I'll leave out my one night stands until you're completely over whatever the hell you think we had."

"I told you that I loved you…" The words rushed out of my mouth.

"I told you that you shouldn't have."

"You can't really be this callous and cold of a person, Andrew…"

"What do you want me to say, Aubrey?" His tone changed. "Your pussy was so magical that it opened my eyes and made me want to change all my ways for you? That I can't live or breathe without knowing that you're by my side? Is that what you're expecting me to say?"

"No." I tried not to cry. "A simple apology for—"

"Kicking your inquisitive ass out of my apartment?" He was glaring at me. "For trying to prevent you from feeling like you do right now? *Fine.* I'm sorry I didn't do it sooner."

I resisted the urge to spit in his face and stepped back. I officially despised him. "You are so not the man I thought you were."

"Good, because I'm sure that man is quite pathetic." He briefly shut his eyes and sighed. "Look, Aubrey…"

"It's *Miss Everhart.*" I hissed as I walked toward the door. "Miss. Fucking. Everhart. But not to worry, you'll never have to worry about using it because you won't be seeing me again."

I slammed the door so hard it rattled the windows on the other side of the hall. I ignored the suspicious look from Jessica as I stormed to the parking lot, and sped all the way to the bank.

I withdrew every dollar out of my savings account, and called the bus depot downtown—asking what the fare was for a one-way ticket to New York City.

"That would be seventy nine eighty six," the operator said. "It's ten dollars cheaper if you buy a roundtrip ticket."

"I won't be needing a round trip ticket." I steered my car into my apartment's lot. "Can you tell me when the next bus leaves?"

"Tonight. Would you like me to book that for you now?"

"Absolutely." I recited my credit card info from memory, and listened as she told me about how I needed to take a walk on the Brooklyn Bridge whenever I had the chance.

The second I hung up, I arranged for a cab and sent a quick text to my roommate: *"Something has come up and I have to move out ASAP…I'll be wiring my half of the remaining rent to our landlord, and I'll find a way to have my belongings shipped to me. I'm leaving my keys under that rose plant in the laundry room—Aubrey."*

Grabbing two large suitcases from my closet, I stuffed them with whatever I could find, and placed Mr. Petrova's recommendation letter into my purse.

As I was writing myself a reminder (*"That asshole still has my panties…Need to shop for more."*), my mother called.

"Yes?" I answered.

"Excuse me, Aubrey?" she said.

I rolled my eyes. "Hello?"

"Much better." There was a smile in her voice. "What time should I expect you at The Grove tonight?"

"Never. I'm not coming."

"Save me your tantrums, Aubrey. There's a lot of money riding on this first dinner. Would you like me and your father to pick you up?"

"I said I'm not coming. Did you not hear me?"

"Aubrey…" She lowered her voice. "I've been trying to hold back for the past few weeks, but you know what? I am sick and tired of you being so damn thoughtless and selfish about your father's aspirations. Neither of us personally give a damn about your thoughts on the election, but since you're a member of this family, I demand that you—"

"Go to hell." I hung up and continued packing, even faster now.

Subject: Cab.

Miss Aubrey Everhart,

Your cab has arrived at the address you specified. It will wait for exactly five minutes.

—Durham Cab Co.

I rushed into the bathroom and filled a plastic bag with toiletries, and then I placed them into my suitcase and headed outside.

"Bus station, right?" The cab driver, a woman, smiled as I approached.

"Yes, please."

She took my bags and placed them into the trunk as I slid into the backseat. I felt my heart hurting with every second that passed, and as much as I tried to block out the thoughts about Andrew, images of his face infiltrated my brain anyway.

I was picturing the last full night we spent together, the night before he kicked me out of his condo, and no matter how hard I tried to make sense of what happened the very next night, I couldn't. All I could do was cry.

My phone vibrated against my knee and I flipped it over, hoping to see Mr. Petrova's name, but it was Andrew.

"Hello?" I answered.

"What are you doing?"

"I have ballet practice on Wednesdays...Shouldn't you know that by now?"

"If you were actually in ballet practice you wouldn't be picking up your phone."

Silence.

"Aubrey?" He sounded concerned. "Are you crying?"

"No." I lied, turning up the volume on my car radio.

"What's wrong?"

"Nothing. I just said—"

"Stop fucking lying to me, Aubrey," he said. "What's wrong with you?"

"I got sent home from practice today."

"Okay. And?"

"There is no 'And' about this..." Tears welled in my eyes. "I've never been sent home before. He made me feel like shit today. He even told the understudy to be prepared to take my place right in front of me, and then he told me not to come back until next week..."

"I've told you the reason why he does that. Why don't you believe me?"

"Because I really was bad today," I admitted. "My feet are swollen and I didn't bandage them properly, so I was off by an eighth of a count for most of the day..."

He sighed. "I'm sure you were still ten times better than everyone else. Don't you think?"

"No..."

"Trust me. I'm pretty sure he's just—"

"Can I come over tonight?" I cut him off, hoping for a yes, but all I heard was silence. I knew I'd pushed my luck the first couple nights we spent together, but I didn't want it to be a rare thing. I wanted more.

"Are you going to give me an answer, Andrew?"

"Yes," he said. "You can come over. Where are you?"

"Outside your door."

He opened it seconds later and looked me up and down, raising his eyebrow. "I would've picked you up."

"I almost asked you to..."

He grabbed my hand and pulled me inside, keeping his eyes locked on mine. As the door shut, he pulled me into his arms and shook his head at me.

"What are you doing, Aubrey?"

"What do you mean?"

"Why do you keep insisting on breaking every rule I have?"

"Why do you keep letting me?"

Without saying another word, his lips were on mine and his hands were sliding around my waist—deftly unbuttoning my skirt, quickly pushing it down to the floor.

His hands grazed my backside, searching for my panties, but there were none.

"Remind me to return your collection." He laughed softly and led me over to the couch.

He dropped my hand and then he sat on the floor, looking up at me. Unzipping his pants, he pulled out a condom and slowly rolled it over his cock.

I started to bend low so I could sit next to him, but he grabbed my thighs.

"Stop," he said. "I don't want you to sit on the floor."

"Okay." I looked over my shoulder. "Do you want me to sit on the coffee table?"

"No..." He trailed his fingers up my legs. "On my face."

"What?"

"Sit your pussy on my face."

I stood still, speechless—unable to process what he'd just asked me to do.

Smirking, he pulled me close and tapped my left leg. "Lift that onto the pillow behind me." He commanded me with his eyes and I slowly lifted my foot and pressed it into the cushion.

"Good girl." He rubbed his hands along the inside of my thighs, blowing kisses against my skin. "Grab onto my hair..."

My hands found their way onto his head as he slipped two fingers inside of me, as he slowly moved them in and out.

He darted his tongue against my clit and groaned. "Are you actually going to follow my directions today?"

"Yes…"

"I need you to be as still as possible." One of his hands cupped my ass, palming it as he continued to stretch my pussy with his fingers. "Can you do that?"

I nodded, letting a low moan escape my mouth.

"Is that a yes?" He didn't give me chance to answer. He drew my swollen clit into his mouth, instantly making my knees buckle beneath me.

Shutting my eyes, I screamed as he gripped my hips and slightly rocked me against his mouth—licking every part of me with his tongue, lapping up every drop.

"Andrew…" I could barely hear my own voice. "Andrew…"

My right leg lost its hold on the floor and I nearly fell forward, but he grabbed me and held me still—not moving his mouth away.

I pulled his hair hard, begging him to slow down, to let me attempt to control the pace, but it was no use.

He continued to fuck me with his mouth, ignoring my every scream.

As my hips jerked and quivers began to race through my body, he wrapped his arms around my legs and slowly pulled me down, lowering me onto his cock.

"Ahhhh…." I breathed as he buried himself inch by inch. "I…I…"

"You, what?" He kissed my forehead once he was entirely inside of me. "Do you not want to ride me this way? Would you prefer if I bent you over?"

I shook my head, and he covered one of my nipples with his mouth, swirling his tongue around it until it hardened.

Without him telling me to, I wrapped my arms around his neck and moved myself up and down his cock.

"Harder..." He bit my neck. "I want you to fuck me as hard as I fuck you..."

I grinded my hips into him again and again, as forceful as I could, but he grabbed me and began thrusting his own hips up from the floor.

"Andrew, I'm going to cum..." I cried out as he completely took over. "I'm going to—"

He slapped my ass as my body finally gave in, as his gave in, too.

Breathless, I leaned against his chest, but he didn't let me rest long. He eased me out of his lap and stood up—walking off to toss away the condom.

Heading back over to me, he scooped me into his arms and carried me into his bedroom, gently lowering me onto his sheets.

I rolled over to the side of the bed I preferred—the side by the window, and waited for him to lay next to me, but he didn't. He took a seat near the edge of the bed and lifted my feet into his lap.

I was too tired to ask him what he was doing, and the next thing I felt was a warm, soothing liquid dripping onto my skin. Then I felt his hands slowly spreading it around the places where the swelling hurt the most.

I moaned as his fingers massaged my soles, said his name as his fingers caressed every tender spot.

"Shhh," he whispered, rendering me speechless as he continued to soothe me.

Every few minutes, he looked back at me and asked, "Would you like me to stop?"

I shook my head and kept my eyes shut, relishing every moment of this.

After what felt like hours of bliss, after he'd given me the best foot massage I'd ever had, he climbed in bed next to me and pulled me against his chest.

"Goodnight, Aubrey," he whispered. "I hope you feel better."

Elated, I threaded my fingers through his hair. "You're not going to insist on taking me home tonight?"

"Not unless you keep talking." He growled. "Go to sleep..."

"Thank you for the foot massage... That was really—"

"Stop talking, Aubrey." He rolled me on top of him. "Go to sleep."

"I was just saying thank you. I can't say thank you?"

"No." He pressed his lips against mine and kissed me until I couldn't breathe, saying, "Don't make me fuck you to sleep," in between breaths.

I attempted to roll over, but his grip was too strong.

Smiling, I positioned my head against his heartbeat and whispered, "Can you hear me? Are you sleeping?"

No answer. Just deep, sleeping breaths.

I hesitated a few seconds. "I love you..."

foreseeable risk (n.):

A danger which a reasonable person should anticipate as the result from his/her actions.

Andrew

"Jessica!" I glanced at the slightly normal looking cup of coffee on my desk.

"Yes, Mr. Hamilton?"

"Could you ask Miss Everhart to come in here, please?" I needed to see her face.

She'd been avoiding me all week, and if all I had to say was "sorry"—whether I actually meant it or not, it was worth it. I missed seeing her seductive mouth in the mornings, remembering how it felt when she pressed it against mine.

"I would do that," Jessica said, "but seeing as though she put in her resignation letter last week, I'm pretty sure that's impossible."

"She *quit*?"

Without telling me?

Jessica raised her eyebrow. "She did. I gave you the letter she left, too. It was quite interesting."

"I never got a letter."

She walked over to my desk and sifted through the clutter.

"Here it is," she said. "She left you two letters…Anything else?"

"No…"

She tilted her head to the side and tapped her lip, looking as if she wanted to say something, but she smiled and left the room.

Locking the door, I tore the first letter open and read it.

Dear GBH,

Thank you very much for hiring me as your undergraduate intern. I've had quite the experience working for you and am honored by all I've learned. However, due to personal reasons, I am resigning as of today.

I apologize for such short notice, and I wish your firm continued success in your future endeavors.

—Aubrey Everhart.

I sighed and opened the other letter that was addressed directly to me.

Dear Mr. Hamilton,
FUCK. YOU.
—Aubrey

overrule (v.):

To reject an attorney's objection to a question of a witness of admission of evidence.

Aubrey

New York City was an entirely different universe. It was nothing like I expected, yet everything I wanted all at once.

The sidewalks were persistently packed with people rushing to get somewhere, the streets were seas of taxis, and the cacophony of sounds—the shouting from the street vendors, the rumbling of the subway below, and the endless chatter between the executives and casual-ites all blended into an almost pleasing melody.

Not that I had much time to listen to it, anyway.

The second I arrived in New York last week, I'd checked into a cheap hotel and rushed to register for the NYCB audition.

Every day for the past week, I jumped out of bed at four in the morning and headed to Lincoln Center to learn the required audition piece—the hardest choreography I'd encountered in my life.

It was faster, choppier, and the instructors refused to show it more than twice a day. There was no conversation outside of tempo counts, no questions were allowed either. On top of that, the company's pianist only elected to play the accompanying music at full speed, never slowing down to make the learning process easier.

There were hundreds of girls vying for a place in the company, and from what I gathered from conversations here or there, most of them were already professionals.

I didn't let that deter me, though.

When the grueling practices came to an end, I took that chance to find a new place in the city to dance on my own: A rooftop in view of Times Square, an abandoned historical store on the Upper East Side, or in front of bookstore windows in the West End.

Despite my immediate love for this city, it wasn't enough to distract me from my heartbreak. Nor was it enough to distract me from the fact that today, official audition day, I was late.

Sweating, I jumped off the subway and ran down Sixty Sixth Street—paying no mind to my burning lungs.

Keep going...Keep going...

A man to my left stepped out of a cab and I immediately jumped in.

"Lincoln Center, please!" I shouted.

"It's right up the street." The driver looked at me through the rearview mirror, confused.

"Please? I'm already late."

He shrugged and pulled off as I tried to steady my breathing.

Not wanting to waste any time, I pulled my black tutu out of my bag and pulled it over my tights. I took out my makeup and applied it the best I could, and as we approached the curb, I tossed a ten dollar bill at the driver and jumped out of the car.

Rushing into the building, I headed straight for the theater, relieved that one of the directors was still standing outside the doors.

"Yes?" She looked me up and down as I approached. "May I help you with something?"

"I'm here for the auditions."

"For the *nine o'clock* auditions?" She looked at her watch. "It's nine fifteen."

"I'm sorry...I called an hour ago and said—"

"Your first cab broke down? That was you?"

I nodded.

She studied me for a few more seconds—pursing her lips. Then she opened the door. "You can change into your whites in the dressing room. Hurry up."

The door shut behind me before I could ask what she meant by "[my] whites," but as my eyes scanned the stage, I realized that every dancer was dressed in a white leotard and matching tutu.

Shit...

My cheeks heated as I looked over my outfit. I didn't have my whites in my bag. They were at home.

Nearing the stage, I set my bag in a chair and tried to ignore that dread that was building inside my chest. I just needed to focus on giving it my all during this routine. That was it.

I found an open spot onstage and stretched my arms—noticing the smirks and whispers that were being thrown in my direction.

Undaunted, I smiled at anyone who made eye contact and continued my routine.

"May I have your attention, please?" A man's voice came over the speaker. "Can everyone stop stretching and make your way to the edge of the stage, please?"

I set my leg down and followed the crowd, finding a spot on the end.

The man addressing us was a tall grey haired man with wiry glasses, and he was the definition of the word "legend": His name was Arnold G. Ashcroft, and I'd followed him and his choreography for years. He was once the most sought after specialist in the world, but when he dropped in the rankings, it was only to his Russian rival: Paul Petrova.

"We're happy to see such a huge turnout for this session of auditions," he said. "As you know, due to a series of unfortunate events, we are overhauling our entire staff. That said, we are keeping our current production schedule as is, which means we will be filling in the roles of principle dancers, soloists, and corps members within the next fourteen days."

"Rehearsals will be long and hard—four to ten, midnight if need be, and there will be no room for excuses or…" He looked me up and down, frowning at my attire. "*Mistakes*."

"This is the first round of six. You will be told of your status once the music stops, and if you are sent home, please don't hesitate to try again next year. I see a lot of failures from last summer, so I'm hoping you've learned something between then and now…"

"For this round, we'll do a portion of the Balanchine routine in groups of eight. You may stretch for a few minutes and then we will begin."

He waved at the man who was taking his seat at the piano, and then he turned around and gave a thumbs up to three people who were sitting in the judge's seats. Smiling, he ascended the stage's steps, and greeted a few familiar faces.

I made my way over and tapped his shoulder.

"Yes?" He turned around.

"Um…" I withered under his intense glare.

"Good morning, Mr. Ashcroft. My name is Aubrey Everhart and I'm—"

"*Late*." He cut me off. "You're also the only performer who isn't wearing the mandatory white."

"Yes, well…" I stammered. "That's why I want to speak with you."

"Oh?"

"I want to know if you would allow me to go home and change."

"And why would I allow that, Miss Everhart?"

"So I can audition with the group this afternoon and be judged fairly. I just think that I've already—"

"Stop." He pressed a pen against my lips. "Ladies, may I please have your attention?"

An immediate silence fell over the theater.

"I want you all to meet *Aubrey Everhart*." He smiled. "She's just informed me that due to the fact that she was late and decided to wear improper attire to her audition today, that there's a chance she'll be judged unfairly."

The ballerina across from me folded her arms.

"Now," he said. "Since the world of ballet is fair and has always been about catering to the needs of the *unprepared*, is there anyone who would have a problem if I allowed Miss Everhart to go home, change, and return for the auditions at six?"

Every dancer on stage raised her hand into the air.

"I thought so." His tone was cold. "If you think a wrongly colored tutu is going to affect how well you perform, you should leave right now."

I swallowed, wishing I could disappear.

"You can dance in the first group." He shook his head at me and walked away.

Disregarding the soft snickering from the other girls, I returned to my former spot on stage and stretched once more. I tried to block out everything that had gone wrong this morning and pretended that I was in Durham again—dancing for one of the best directors in the world.

"Miss Everhart?" A woman said my name, snapping me out of my thoughts.

"Yes?"

"Are you going to take your place at center stage with everyone else, or do you need more time to find it?"

I smiled at the judge's table and stepped into the line.

The woman signaled to the pianist and he played the B-flat scale before starting the piece. As his fingers forced the notes, my arms went high above my head and I slowly spun around on my toes—wincing as my right pointe slipper cracked.

I ignored the pain and continued the routine. Terribly.

Each time I attempted a jump, I landed off balance and slipped an eighth of a count behind everyone else. My turns were awkward—frantically paced, and my pointe work was so choppy that I bumped into the girl next to me.

Embarrassed, I murmured sorry and spun around, but I lost my balance and fell onto the stage. Headfirst.

I ignored the loud outburst of laughter from the dancers in the audience and stood up, attempting to fall back into the routine.

"Stop!" Mr. Ashcroft bellowed from the side of the stage, making the notes come to an end.

He walked in front of our line and stepped directly in front of me.

"I just looked through your file, Miss Everhart." He looked unimpressed. "You recently studied under Mr. Petrova?"

I nodded.

"Use your words, please."

"Yes…" I cleared my throat. "Yes, I did."

"And he wrote an actual recommendation letter on your behalf?"

"Yes sir."

He looked at me in utter disbelief. Shock. "You expect me to believe that when you dance so stiffly? When you're a count behind each and every step?"

"Yes…" My voice was a whisper.

"Well…At least you can always say that you studied under one of the greatest choreographers of all time. You can leave my theater now."

My heart sank. "*What*?"

"I don't think you're a good fit for our company. We'll email you this evening with a link to purchase discounted tickets for the season's shows."

A tear rolled down my face, and as if he could see that he'd just broken my heart, he patted my shoulder.

"I can tell that you've had training," he said. "Very good training. And I can see that you have potential, but we're not interested in *potential* here. For the rest of you, congratulations! You've earned yourselves a spot in the next round of auditions. Now, please clear the stage so the next group of dancers may perform."

A loud applause arose from the hopefuls in the audience, and I felt as if I was watching my life fall apart in front of me. Hurt, I followed the dancers to the side steps—unsure of what to do next.

Grabbing my bag, I avoided the pathetic glances of the hopefuls and shook my head.

"That just goes to show you," Mr. Ashcroft said to the other panelists, laughing, "even Petrova picks duds sometimes."

I turned around.

Enraged, I marched up the stage's steps and took a seat on the white line. I untied my right slipper and prepared another one—bending it forward and backward until it felt right.

"You can change your shoes in the restroom, Miss Everhart." Mr. Ashcroft chided. "The stage is for actual performers. Or did Petrova not teach you that?"

"I need another chance," I said. "Just because I didn't nail the Balanchine piece that doesn't make me a bad dancer."

"Of course it doesn't, honey." He mocked me. "It makes you a *failed dancer*, who is currently using my stage and sucking up precious audition time for those who might actually make the cut in my company."

I walked over to the pianist. "Tchaikovsky, *Swan Lake*. Act two, scene fourteen. Do you know that piece?"

"Umm…" He looked confused.

"Do you know it or not?"

"Yes, but—" He pointed to another judge who was now standing and crossing her arms.

"Could you please play it?" I pleaded with my eyes. "It's only three minutes long."

He let out a sigh and straightened his back, strumming the keys of the piano. With no count off, he played the first few notes of the concerto and the softs sounds echoed off the theater's walls.

"Miss Everhart, you're wasting everyone's time..." Mr. Ashcroft's face turned red as I slipped into fifth position.

I could hear him sighing and tsk-ing, could hear the other hopefuls murmuring, but as I twirled around the stage and transitioned from an arabesque to a grand jete, their talking stopped.

The notes lingered longer—darker, as the song progressed and I made sure each motion of my hands was smooth and graceful. As I leapt across the stage and completed a series of perfect pirouettes, I could see Mr. Ashcroft rubbing his chin.

Before I knew it, I was in a trance and I was dancing in the middle of Times Square, underneath flashing lights and a star-filled sky.

I continued dancing long after the last note, humming the additional refrain that most pianists ignored, and I ended by leaning forward on my left leg—holding my right one in the air behind me.

The panelists stared back at me. Their faces expressionless.

"Are you done, Miss Everhart?" Mr. Ashcroft asked.

"Yes..."

"Good. Now, get the hell off my stage."

I stood upright and bit my lip to prevent myself from breaking down in front of them.

"Thank you very much for the opportunity..." I grabbed my bag and rushed off stage—running down the hallway and outside the building.

I stopped in front of a trashcan and bent over, waiting for the inevitable vomit.

Deep down I knew that I was a good dancer—that I'd just danced my heart out, and I honestly felt like I deserved a second chance.

The thought of failing had never crossed my mind when I signed up for this audition, and the option of returning to Durham was too painful to bear.

Heaving, I tearfully weighed my options: 1) Go home and rejoin Mr. Petrova's dance program. 2) Go back inside and tell the panel they're all fucking idiots, or—

"Miss Everhart?" Someone tapped my shoulder.

I spun around, finding myself face to face with a stoic Mr. Ashcroft.

"Yes?" I wiped my face on my sleeve and forced a smile.

"What you just did on stage was rude, unprofessional, and *horrible*. It was the worst thing I have ever seen a prospective dancer do and I didn't appreciate it all…That said, be here *on time* for the second round next week."

My jaw dropped and I didn't get a chance to scream or say thank you.

He was already gone.

I pulled out my phone, anxious to tell someone that I'd made it to the next round, but I had no one to call.

All I had were angry texts from my parents, tons of their missed calls, and I knew better than to reach out to them right now. They didn't really give a damn.

I searched for Mr. Petrova's number—hoping I'd saved it, but an email from Andrew appeared on my screen.

Subject: Your Resignation.

I was tempted to open it, but my heart wouldn't let me do it. He was the main reason why I fled here, and I didn't need him intruding on my new life.

I deleted his message and decided that I wasn't going to think about him anymore. All that mattered now was ballet.

months later…

rebuttal (n.):

Evidence introduced to counter, disprove or contradict the opposition's evidence or a presumption, or responsive legal argument.

Andrew

The fall season came and went, taking the changing leaves and amber sunsets with it. New interns filled the positions at GBH, new cases and clients packed the calendars, and as winter enveloped the city, one thing remained clear: Durham was only one step above the shit ladder when compared to New York City.

At least when it came to the winter, anyway.

This was the coldest winter the city had experienced, and since it was a Southern town, they were ill-prepared. The courtroom I was currently sitting in featured blankets lined against the windows instead of proper insulation, and there were space heaters jutting from every outlet.

There were few salt trucks available to control the icy streets, even fewer people who actually knew how to drive in such weather, and for whatever reason, there were no more suitable women available.

"Andrew?" Mr. Bach tapped my shoulder. "The prosecution is done with the witness…Are you going to redirect? That last line might have influenced the jury."

"Permission to redirect, Your Honor." I stood up from the table.

The judge nodded and I stared at the woman on the stand. She'd been lying through her teeth since this trial began and I'd had enough.

"Miss Everhart—" I cleared my throat. "I mean, *Miss Everly*, do you believe that leaving your husband in his time of need was what was best for your company?"

"Yes," she said. "I told you that during our first meeting."

"No." I shook my head. "You told me that you loved him and that your sole reasoning for leaving him was because you thought he didn't love you back. Is that not true?"

"It is, but—"

"So, because he didn't say that he loved you on *your terms*, because he told you he was actually incapable of loving you that way, you decided to leave him. Didn't you?"

"No…I left him because he was spending the company's money on unnecessary things and cheating on me."

"Did you ever think about *his feelings*?" I asked. "Did you think to simply ask if your leaving would affect him—whether you were on good terms or not?"

"He was…" She was breaking down. "He was cheating on me…"

"Was he? Or did you just want more than what he was willing to give you emotionally, Miss Everly?"

"Please stop…"

"Is it possible that you could be making all of this up?"

"No, never. I would never—"

"Is it possible that you're a *fucking liar*?"

"Order! Order!" The judge banged her gavel and the jury gasped. "Counsel, my chambers. NOW!"

I stared at the fake tears falling down Miss Everly's face. This case was a wrap.

I walked into the judge's chambers and shut the door. "Yes, Your Honor?"

"Are you out of your goddamn mind?"

"Excuse me?"

"You just called your own witness a fucking liar."

I looked through the window, seeing that the bailiff was handing her a box of Kleenex.

"Are you on a new prescription?" she asked. "Drinking? Smoking something other than Cubans?"

"Because I'm having one bad day in court?"

"Because you've had *several* bad days in court."

"I don't recall calling any of my other witnesses fucking liars…"

"You called for an objection during the reading of a verdict."

"Maybe I didn't like the sound of it."

"Maybe, but you never mess up in my court." She paused. "*Ever*…Please go get yourself checked out, Mr. Hamilton. I'd really hate to be the judge presiding over your very first loss."

She motioned for me to follow her out of her chambers. She took a seat in her chair and announced that the current trial was being postponed due to a rare rule brought up by the defense, and that we would reconvene two weeks from now.

Relieved, I closed my briefcase and ignored a red-faced Miss Everly.

"Mr. Bach," she said, glaring at me, "I would really like for us to win this case, so could you please—"

"It's already taken care of," he said, cutting her off. "No worries." He gave her a reassuring smile and asked Mr. Greenwood to walk her out to her car. Then he turned and looked at me.

"Andrew, Andrew, Andrew…" He sighed. "I think you need some time off. I'll take over this case, alright? And Mr. Greenwood and I will be in contact with any of your clients who have cases within the next few weeks."

"You're overreacting," I said. "It's one fucking case."

"One fucking case that you're on the verge of losing."

"I *never* lose."

"I know." He patted me on the shoulder. "Go home, Andrew. You've actually never taken a vacation anyway. Maybe it's what you need right now."

"No." I grabbed my briefcase. "I'll see you at the Reber consultation tomorrow morning."

He called after me, but I ignored him. I sped back to GBH, prepared to immerse myself in more work. I was avoiding my condo as much as possible lately; I could hardly stand to be there.

Unopened condoms lined my wet bar—a reminder of how long it'd been since I had pussy, empty liquor bottles lined all of my window sills, and my Cuban cigar selection was long gone.

"Are you okay, Mr. Hamilton?" the main secretary asked as I walked through the firm's doors.

I ignored her. Too many people were asking me that question lately and I was tired of hearing it.

I shut myself inside my office and pulled my phone's chord out of the wall. I didn't need any distractions.

For the rest of the morning, I read over my files in utter silence—not even answering emails from my own clients.

"Jessica!" I called her once the clock struck noon. "*Jessica*!"

"Yes, Mr. Hamilton?" She walked in right away.

"Is there any reason why you suddenly decided to stop organizing my case files by date?" I slid a folder across the desk. "Any reason why *you've* decided to stop doing your goddamn job?"

"You think I actually have time to organize all your case files by date? Do you know how long that takes?" She raised her eyebrow. "That was *Miss Everhart's* idea. I told her it was a waste of time, but I guess not. If I have some free hours in between the Doherty case next week I'll try to do that."

"Thank you." I ignored the fact that my heart skipped a beat when she said Miss Everhart. "You can get out of my office now."

I pulled the papers from the file and began reorganizing them. As I clipped all of the witness testimonies together, Jessica cleared her throat.

"You miss her, don't you?" she asked.

"Excuse me?" My head shot up.

"Aubrey," she said, smiling. "You miss her, don't you?"

I said nothing. I just watched as she sauntered over to me, slowly raising the sides of her skirt to show that she wasn't wearing anything underneath.

Smiling, she picked up my coffee cup and took a long, dramatic sip.

"*Jessica...*" I groaned.

"You don't have to admit to it." She plopped her bare ass atop my desk. "But it's clear that you haven't been yourself for quite a while..."

"Are your ass cheeks touching my desk right now?"

"You don't even insult me the normal way that you used to," she said. "I actually miss that."

I pulled out a box of Clorox wipes.

"She doesn't stay in her old apartment anymore, you know. I think she moved."

"What makes you think I care about where an ex-employee lives?"

"Because the address you gave me for that envelope and red box delivery belonged to her."

"That was for an old friend."

"Yeah, well..." She slid off my desk. "Your old friend must share an address with Aubrey Everhart because I pulled up her records from HR and she definitely stayed there."

Silence.

"I thought so." She smirked. "So, since you and I are so close—"

"We are *not* close."

"It's my duty as a friend to let you know that you're really letting yourself go..." She actually looked saddened. "You're not shaving, you're coming to work every morning reeking of alcohol, and you're barely yelling at the interns...I haven't had a wet dream about you in a very long time."

I rolled my eyes and stood up, wiping the part of my desk where her ass had been.

"But, since I know your secret about Aubrey now, you can know one of mine," she said, lowering her voice. "Sometimes, in the mornings, when she would bring you your coffee and shut the door, I would stand outside and listen..." Her eyes lit up. "And I would just pretend that it was me..."

"Pretend *what* was you?"

"Aubrey," she said. "Clearly she was good enough for you to break the 'I don't fuck my employees' rule." She stepped toward the door. "I knew the second she started here that you liked her."

"You have no idea what you're talking about."

"Of course I don't." She looked over her shoulder. "But I do know that the second she quit, you've been a shell of yourself. You have yet to realize that you've been wearing the same blue suit for two weeks straight."

I took a long swig of scotch from the bottle, numbly staring at the images that were playing on my television screen. A little blond girl playing in the rain—stomping her red boots in every puddle she could find.

"It's time to go, Emma..."

I winced at hearing the sound of my old voice, but I continued watching the scene.

"Five more minutes!" She begged with a smile.

"You don't even know what that means. You've just heard me say it..."

"Five more minutes!" She jumped into another puddle, laughing. "Five more minutes, Daddy!"

"It's going to rain all week. Don't you want to go home and—"

"*No*!" She stomped her feet in a puddle again, splashing me. And then she smiled innocently into the camera before running away—begging me to chase her.

I couldn't bear to watch anymore. I turned off the TV and knocked the DVD player to the floor.

Fuck...

Walking down the hallway, I straightened the "E" and "H" frames that hung on the wall—trying my best not to look too hard.

I didn't need to make myself another drink tonight. I needed someone to talk to.

I grabbed my phone from the night-stand, scrolling down my contacts for the one person who'd once kept the nightmares at bay. Aubrey.

It rang four times and went to voicemail.

"Hi. You've reached Aubrey Everhart," it said. "I'm unable to take your call right now, but if you leave your name and number I'll get back to you as soon as I can."

The second the beep sounded I hung up. Then I called again, just to listen to that small snippet of her voice. I told myself that I wasn't being pathetic by calling her five times—knowing damn well that she wasn't there, but when I called the sixth time, she picked up.

"Hello?" she answered. "*Andrew*?"

"Hello, Aubrey..."

"What do you want?" Her voice was cold.

"How are you?"

"What do you want, Andrew?" she asked, even colder. "I'm busy."

"Then why did you pick up?"

"It was a mistake." She ended the call.

I drew in a sharp breath, shocked that she hung up on me. I started to type up an email, chastising her for being so rude, but I noticed that she hadn't responded to my last three in months:

Subject: Your Resignation.

Even though the last two words of your resignation letter were ridiculous and unprofessional, I'd like to take you up on your offer to fuck you.

Name the time.
—Andrew.

Subject: My Suit.

Since you have yet to pick up your final check, should I assume that's your way of letting me keep it to replace the suit you ruined?

—Andrew.

Subject: BALLET.

I stopped by your dance hall earlier. You weren't there.

Did you quit that, too?

—Andrew.

I decided that I needed to replace her. Fast.

I grabbed my laptop from my nightstand and logged into LawyerChat, looking for another Alyssa-type.

I spent all night roaming the chat rooms, answering questions left and right—gauging the personalities of the askers, but none of them grabbed me. Still, one woman who was listed as a high profile lawyer with ten years of experience seemed promising, so I clicked on her chat box.

"If you have ten years of experience, what could you possibly need help with on this site?" I typed.

"You're never too old to learn new things…Why are you on here?"

"I'm looking for a replacement."

"You're trolling for an employee?"

"No, just someone I can talk to and make cum occasionally."

She blocked me.

I tried talking to a few other women—keeping my true words to myself, but ultimately they just wanted to use me for information. They weren't open to talking about anything else, and since LawyerChat had expanded its site recently, there seemed to be an influx of law students using it as a complaint board about their professors.

I shut the laptop and took another swig from my bottle—immediately realizing that there was only *one* "Alyssa-type": Aubrey…

Maybe I made a mistake…

Out the corner of my eye I spotted an envelope under the slit of my door. It hadn't been there when I first arrived home, and it hadn't been there a few hours ago when I ordered my dinner.

Confused, I walked over and picked it up.

It was an official court summons to testify in a New York hearing, but it wasn't addressed to my new name. It was addressed to Liam Henderson.

remedy (n.):

The means to achieve justice in any matter in which legal rights are involved.

Aubrey

The Firebird.
Jewels.
Swan Lake.

I wrote down the roles I wanted to audition for in my planner, smiling as I ran my hands across my acceptance letter for the umpteenth time. I had ten copies of it—two of them were framed, seven were for inspiration whenever I was feeling down, and one was for my parents. (I just hadn't had the time or energy to draft an "I fucking told you so" letter to mail with it.)

I looked at the clock on my wall and checked my phone, trying to suppress the butterflies that were fluttering around my stomach.

The guy I was now dating, Brian—a fellow dancer in the company, was supposed to call me with something important he wanted to talk about.

Ever since I met him, he'd been trying his hardest to woo me—taking me on dates in between rehearsals, joining me as I danced on rooftops and icy park benches. He was kind, sweet, funny, and the perfect example of what it meant to be a gentleman.

He was like the nice guy in the Old Hollywood movies, the type that held your hand for no reason at all, the type that walked you to your door and waited until you were completely inside before stepping away. He was the type that kissed you—softly and tenderly, whispering that he liked your lips, but never taking things any further.

In other words, he was nothing like Andrew.

Nothing like.

Even though his kisses never left me panting and wet, and his touches never set my nerves on fire, he never made me feel like shit.

My phone vibrated and I looked at the screen. Brian.

"Did you receive the roses I sent you today?"

I grinned, looking over at the red and white blooms on my fireplace.

"Yes." I texted back. "Thank you very much. I love them."

"I placed something else in the vase for you, too…You should use it to relax tonight. I'll be calling you after I get out of rehearsal."

"Looking forward to it." I added a smiley face at the end of my text and walked over to the vase, lifting the flowers up by their stems. There was a huge packet of pink bath beads and rose petals with a handwritten note across the front:

"The next time you take a bath…Think about me…
—Brian"

My heart fluttered and I couldn't help but want to immediately take him up on the idea. I slipped out of my clothes and headed into the bathroom, tossing the beads under rushing water.

As I let down my hair, I turned the volume on my ringer to the highest setting, and before I could set it down, I noticed a new email. Andrew.

My heart nearly jumped out of my chest, as it always did when one of his sporadic emails or calls graced my screen.

Everything in me told me not to open it, to continue ignoring him, and to let him feel just how alone and underappreciated I felt months ago, but I couldn't help it.

Subject: Thoreau & Alyssa.

You once said that you missed when we were Thoreau and Alyssa because I supposedly treated you better. I don't think I treated you any differently. I just really wanted to fuck you. But when we did meet in person, I unfortunately wanted to fuck you even more.

I personally prefer us as "Andrew & Aubrey" because on a night like tonight, when there's nothing I would rather do than fuck you against my balcony until you cum, at least I can actually picture what your pussy feels like and no longer have to imagine.

Pick up the phone...
—Andrew

I shook my head and set the phone down, mentally erasing that message and stepping into the tub.

I lay back and let the hot water rise to my chest, exhaling as it warmed my skin.

It was becoming easier to avoid thinking about Andrew now that I was talking to Brian, but it was harder trying to force myself to forget. I still thought about him late at night when I was in my bed, often wishing he was inside of me.

Nonetheless, I wasn't running back to him and his asshole-ish ways, and I would never allow him to come back to me.

Never.

I scrubbed myself clean with a soft loofah, trying my best to ignore the intense throbbing between my legs that always came when thinking about Andrew. I filled a ladle with water and poured it over my head—unable to push away the thought of Andrew washing my hair in the tub, of him telling me to stand underneath the streams and hold the wall as he grabbed my waist and fucked me from behind.

My fingers found their way to my clit as I remembered him bending me over the vanity in his bathroom, saying "I need you to fucking take it…All of it…" as he palmed my breasts and kissed his way down my spine.

I rubbed my clit in circles—shutting my eyes as I pictured his lips on mine, moaning as it swelled with every caress.

"Ahhhh…." I felt my nipples hardening as the water cooled, and I was close—so close, to coming, but my phone rang.

Andrew?

I immediately stood up and wrapped myself in a robe, rushing to answer it—telling myself that I could pick up his call "just this once."

"Hello?" I held the phone up to my ear without looking at the screen.

"*Aubrey*?" It was Brian.

"Hi…" I sighed, trying to mask my discontent. "How are you?"

"Is this a bad time? You sound kind of upset."

"I'm not upset. I was just getting out of the bath."

"Oh, well good," he said. "Did you use the relaxation kit I bought you?"

"I did."

"Did you also think about me?"

"Yes…" I lied, feeling slightly guilty. "How was rehearsal?"

I walked to my dresser and slipped into a T-shirt, listening to him recount the many ways that Mr. Ashcroft was the devil reincarnate.

"He's worse than Mr. Petrova." I pulled my hair into a ponytail.

"Worse than Paul Petrova?" He laughed. "I don't believe you. I've seen that man's documentary, seen him make grown men cry."

"Well, maybe years ago. Don't get me wrong, he's still rude and overbearing, but he has a layer of softness that Mr. Ashcroft lacks."

"I'll take your word for it…" He cleared his throat. "How tired are you right now?"

"Not too tired, shockingly."

"Well…I wanted to talk to you tonight because I needed to know if you wanted to try something new in our relationship."

"Sure." I climbed into bed. "What is it?"

"Phone sex…" His voice became deeper. "Have you ever done that before?"

I held back a laugh and quickly took off my shirt, tossing it to the floor. "Yes."

"Would you want to do it with me? Like, right now?"

"Yes." I grabbed my vibrator from a box and slipped under the covers, happy that I wouldn't need to think about Andrew to have an orgasm anymore. "Yes, I would like that very much."

"Good," he said. "Well…"

Silence.

"Well, *what*? Are you there, Brian?"

"Sorry, I was taking off my shorts." He hesitated. "So, what are you wearing?"

"Nothing…I'm naked."

"You're naked, Aubrey?" He sounded as if he didn't believe me. "Are you sure you've had phone sex before? This is the part where you're supposed to tell me that you have on lingerie. Work with me, please."

"Okay…I'm wearing a black thong and a black—"

"No, not black. I don't like black. Try blue, navy blue."

"Okay, it's a navy blue thong and a blue bra."

"Yeah, that's more like it. Now, take off the panties with one hand."

I lay there motionless, not sure as to whether I should turn on my vibrator or not.

"Now, imagine me..." He groaned. "Imagine me impaling you with my cock—so deep inside of you, so deep..."

I sighed.

"Can you picture it?" His voice became hoarse. "I need you to picture it...and touch your vagina."

"*What*?"

"Your vagina. Touch it."

I stood up and put on a pair of pajama pants.

"Are you touching it, babe?"

"Ohhh yeah..." I pulled a sweater over my head. "I'm touching my *vagina*..."

"Are you thinking about me licking your folds? Running my tongue along your ass crack?"

"Brian, you're actually..." I shook my head. "You're breaking up..."

"I'm going to stroke you down real good with my tongue, babe. Then I'm going to ram my cock into you again and again—never stopping even if you say no...You can't say no..."

I grabbed a sheet of paper and crumpled it next to the phone. "I can't hear you anymore, Brian...Reception in my bedroom is getting really bad...." I hung up in the middle of his panting and scrolled through my old emails—breaking down and reading the old messages from Andrew, the only man who could ever make me cum with words...

Whether I hated him or not, I needed a release and I knew this was the only way...

stay (n.):

A court-ordered short-term delay in judicial proceedings.

Andrew

"Mr. Hamilton?" The flight attendant tapped my shoulder. "All of the other passengers have departed the plane sir. Thank you for flying first class, and I hope you enjoy New York."

"I'll try." I stood up and grabbed my briefcase from the overhead bin.

I'd tried to get out of coming here for weeks, but it was to no avail. The second I booked my ticket, I canceled all of my consultations and meetings, asked for an extension on my current case, and packed one suitcase. Just one.

I didn't need to be in this city longer than a day, and I refused to even testify. I was going to submit a written testimony to the judge and immediately return to Durham.

As I walked through the airport, I noticed that a few things had changed, but not as much as I'd hoped. People still walked at a breakneck pace, the air still reeked of failure, and the top newspaper was still *The New York Times*.

I placed a few dollars into the paper machine, twisting the key so it could spit out my copy, and then I flipped to the middle section where the justice pieces were kept.

There it was. Section C. The story that covered the entire page:

Another Hearing in the Ongoing Hart Trial: Henderson to Testify This Week

I skimmed the article, slightly impressed that the journalist was writing facts this time and not smearing my name for the hell of it.

I also noticed there were still no pictures of me.

Figures…

"Over here, Mr. Hamilton!" A brunette waved as I stepped off the escalator. "Over here!"

I walked over and she held out her hand.

"I'm Rebecca Waters, lead attorney."

"I know who you are." I offered her a firm shake. "How fast can we get to the judge's chambers?"

"The judge's chambers?" She raised her eyebrow. "I'm supposed to check you into the hotel so we can discuss your testimony…You're supposed to stay here for a couple weeks."

"My return flight leaves in fifteen hours."

She looked shocked. "You only want to submit a written testimony? After all this time?"

"I find it quite impressive that you know how to listen and comprehend at the same time." I looked at my watch. "Where is the town car?"

She groaned and led me down the bustling terminal, through the gates, and into the executive car lot. She was babbling about how "important" this case was, how it would finally close a chapter on my life, but I wasn't listening.

My mind was literally counting the seconds I had left in this place.

"Good morning, sir." The driver grabbed my bag as we approached the car. "I hope you enjoy your stay in New York City."

I nodded and slipped into the back seat, rolling my eyes when Rebecca sat next to me.

"Could you at least stay for one night and think about this, Liam?"

"What did you just call me?"

"I'm sorry," she said. "Andrew...I mean, Mr. Hamilton. Could you at least think about it?"

"I just did."

"Fine." She pulled out her phone, and I looked out the window as the car coasted through the city.

I winced as we passed a billboard where my old firm once held an advertisement, shut my eyes when we passed Emma's favorite toy store.

"Mr. Hamilton..." Rebecca tapped my shoulder. "As a lawyer, I'm sure you know how much more compelling an oral testimony can be over a written one. I am begging you to reconsider this."

"And I'm begging you to get over it." I looked her directly in the eyes. "He and Ava ruined my life and I don't have shit to gain by sitting in a courtroom full of strangers and explaining how. You want an emotional testimony? Hire a fucking drama student to read my words to the jury."

"Things have changed. It's not like it was six years ago."

"That's why *The New York Times* still won't print my picture?"

"They won't print your picture because they think you're an asshole." She snapped. "You also won a huge and expensive case against them years ago or have you suddenly forgotten that? Take it as a compliment that they're even mentioning you in a positive light." She tossed yesterday's paper into my lap. "They even ran that piece. Looks pretty damn good to me."

I picked up the paper and brought it close to my face, and before I could read the article, two words caught my eye: Aubrey Everhart.

Her name was at the bottom of the page, mixed in with several others, in a beautiful black ad:

The New York Ballet Company to Celebrate New Cast Members with Saturday Night Gala.

Tomorrow…

“I just…” Rebecca was still talking. “I just think you should at least stay for a night, clear your head, and really think about this.”

“I’ll stay until tomorrow.”

“Really?” Her eyes lit up.

“Yes.” I stared at Aubrey’s name again. “*Really.*”

harass (v.):

Systematic and/or continual unwanted and annoying pestering, which often includes threats and demands.

Andrew

The prosecutor shook my hand over coffee and tea the next night, batting her light brown eyes.

"Thank you so much for agreeing to stay for a few weeks, Andrew," she said. "This is going to be a real help in this case."

"I'm sure…" I stood up and walked over to the window, looking at the snow covered streets below.

"Your old partner has definitely hired the best lawyers money can buy, and has paid fines and suffered penalties for years, but I think we can finally send him to prison with the new evidence that we have. That, and your testimony, of course."

I said nothing.

"I'm not sure how you would feel about this, but…" Her voice trailed off, and seconds later she was by my side. "Would you like to catch up on all we've missed since you've been gone?"

"Excuse me?"

She rubbed my shoulder. "You left New York and you never looked back. You didn't call anyone or keep in touch…We were such good friends and you—"

"Okay." I cut her off and grabbed her hand, moving it away. "First of all, *no*, I do not want to catch up on shit. I don't give a damn about what I've missed." I looked her up and down. "But from the look of things, it hasn't been much. Second of all, yes, we *were* friends. Past tense. You didn't call or keep in touch with me when everyone in this city was dragging my name through the mud, did you?"

Her cheeks reddened.

"You didn't even call to ask me if the rumors were fucking true." I pointed to the door. "So, please don't think that just because I've agreed to help put an asshole where he belongs, that you and I are, or will ever be friends."

"I'm so sorry…"

"It's six years too late for that." I turned around. "I'll be in court when I'm needed. You can leave now."

I waited until I heard the sound of the door close and called the town-car driver. "What time do I need to leave for the gala if I want to be there once it starts?"

"Now, sir."

I hung up and slipped into my coat, taking the penthouse's private elevator to the lobby. Rushing through the hotel's exit doors, I spotted the car across the street and headed over.

"We should be there in about thirty minutes, Mr. Hamilton." He looked at me through the rearview mirror. "Are you meeting a date at this event tonight?"

"No," I said. "Why are you asking?"

"Because if you were, I was going to suggest that we stop at the floral stand that's three blocks down."

"We can stop." I looked out the window as he pulled off.

I'd thought about telling Aubrey that I was in town, or "good luck" for her performance tonight, but I didn't see a point. Besides, last night, in a moment of weakness, I sent her a rather vague email and her rare response didn't encourage further conversation.

Subject: Happiness.
Are you happy with your current life away from GBH?
Are you pursuing your ballet dreams finally?
—Andrew

Subject: Re: Happiness.
Please stop emailing me and delete my number.
Thank you.
—Aubrey

"Mr. Hamilton?" The driver held the door open. "We've arrived…Do you plan on getting out of the car?"

"Thank you." I grabbed the bouquet of roses and lilies off the seat and gave him a tip, telling him that I needed him to stay close, that I may be bringing someone else back with me.

The line to enter the venue was wrapped around the block, so I skipped everyone and walked straight through the front door.

"Excuse me, sir?" An usher immediately stepped in front of me. "There's a line outside for a reason."

"I don't like to wait."

"None of us do sir," he said, crossing his arms, "but that's gala policy unless you already have a ticket. Do you have a ticket?"

"I don't like those either."

He unclipped a radio from his belt buckle. "Sir, please don't make me call security. You have to purchase a ticket just like everyone else, and you have to stand in line just like everyone else. Now, I'm going to kindly ask you to—"

He stopped mid-sentence once I handed him a clip of hundred dollar bills. "Did you say your ticket was in the front row, sir?"

"Yes. That's exactly what my ticket says."

He smiled and led me down the hall, into a colossal room that featured floor to ceiling windows, glimmering chandeliers, and freshly polished marble floors. Hundreds of tables were dressed in white table cloths—stamped with lavish gold and silver centerpieces, and the letters "NYCB" were etched onto every dinner menu and program.

There was no formal stage in this room, only a slightly elevated platform that stood in the center—in perfect view for all the dinner tables.

"Will this seat be okay for you, sir?" The usher waved his hand over a seat that was directly in front of the platform.

"Yes, thank you."

"Dinner will be served in about an hour, the sponsors of the NYCB will be honored shortly after, and then the short tributes and the dance portion of the gala will begin."

I thanked him again as I took my seat. If I had known the exact order of the program beforehand, I would've shown up much later.

Picking up the brochure in front of me, I flipped through the pages—stopping when I saw Aubrey's face.

Her picture was taken mid-laugh, as she tossed her hair over her shoulder and looked directly into the camera. According to the picture, her hair was much shorter now—it barely touched her shoulders, and her eyes looked more hopeful and happy than I'd ever seen them.

I stared at the picture long and hard, noting all her new changes.

The lights in the room flickered, and a soft applause arose as a woman dressed in all-white stepped onto the platform.

"We will begin now," she said. "Thank you ladies and gentlemen for attending the Annual New York City Ballet Company Gala. It is with great honor and pride that we present tonight's artists—principle dancers, soloists, and corps members. As you know, due to quite a few unfortunate circumstances, we had to replace nearly ninety percent of our group over the past few months, but as always, the show must go on. And, I truly believe that this is the best class we've had in a very long time."

The audience clapped.

"Our company will be performing several productions this year, but the ones that will be presented this winter are *The Firebird*, *Jewels*, and our company favorite, *Swan Lake*."

More applause.

"Tonight, our corps will introduce themselves to you personally and perform small tributes as a thank you for your continued support of the arts. And as always, when it comes to the art of dance, please do not applaud until after the last note has played. Thank you." She walked away and the lights transformed from a stark white to an airy blue, then they dissolved into heavy hues of purple and pink.

One by one, the dancers came out—reciting a short monologue and dancing to a short piece of piano music. While most of the performers were entertaining, a few of them made me wonder if they'd simply awoken this morning and decided try ballet for the first time.

In between the sets, I could hear a few murmurs from the crowd: "Are they sure this is their best cohort?" "Maybe they should've canceled the season after that accident..." "Hopefully, they'll be having nonstop rehearsals until the season actually begins..."

A man next to me was whispering about how he missed "the good old days of the company" when Aubrey stepped onto the floor.

She was wearing a thin black top and a pink tutu, and her lips were coated in a deep dark red.

"Good evening, New York City," she said. "My name is Aubrey Everhart, and..."

She was saying something else, something that made the audience clap loudly, but I could only focus on how good she looked. I'd never admit it to anyone, but I'd kept that photo frame of us on my nightstand ever since she left—looking at her pretty face at night whenever I had a bad day.

Tonight she wasn't "pretty," though. She was a fucking vision.

Her mouth stopped moving amidst another round of applause from the audience, and the soft sounds of a piano and harp slowly filled the room.

Aubrey shut her eyes and started her routine, dancing as if she was the only person here.

There was an immediate change in the gala's atmosphere. Everyone watching her was fully engaged—captivated, by her every move.

Out of nowhere, a male dancer joined her, picking her up and holding her high above his head—spinning her around as the music became harsher. After he set her down, the two of them completed steps together—smiling at each other and exchanging glances that made it clear that they knew each other a little too well.

The second the music stopped, the male dancer pulled her into his arms and kissed her lips.

What the fuck...

The crowd stood to its feet and clapped for the first time all night, but I remained seated, completely taken aback by what the fuck I just saw.

"Maybe I won't have to cancel my season tickets after all, eh?" The man next to me winked. "Bravissimo!"

I narrowed my eyes at Aubrey and her partner, seething as he wrapped an arm around her waist and strummed his fingers against her skin. He whispered into her ear and she blushed, making my blood pressure soar to an all-time high.

"Well, what a response!" The director took the floor. "Thank you, Miss Everhart and Mr. Williams. I want you all to know that those two will be headlining next month's Silver Moon Gala as well..." She continued talking, saying more about the program, but her words were soundless to me.

I was confused by what I just saw—not sure if Aubrey's mouth had actually been on someone else.

More dancers took the floor, more applause, more speeches, and my thoughts remained the same. It wasn't until the patrons took the floor, that I realized that the showcase part of this evening was over.

"Are you interested in donating to the NYCB?" A ballerina, still dressed in her white performance outfit, stepped in front of me. "Would you like to make a contribution?"

"My *contribution* was the ticket I bought for tonight." I stood up, leaving the flower bouquet behind, and walked off in search of Aubrey.

It didn't take long to find her.

Dressed in a rather revealing silver dress, she was in a corner laughing with her male dancer friend, batting her eyes as he handed her a drink.

"Excuse me, sir?" Someone tapped me on the shoulder.

"Yes?" I kept my eyes on Aubrey.

"Um, if you stay for the after-portion of the event, you have to donate…It's part of the rules. It was written in bold so—"

"Here." I handed her whatever bills were left in my wallet.

She disappeared.

Aubrey's friend kissed her forehead and stepped away, giving me the perfect opportunity to approach, but she was swarmed by a group of other ballerinas.

Friends, it seemed.

I waited for their conversation to end, until she told them she'd join them later, and then I made my move.

As she turned around, I placed my hand on her shoulder—feeling a jolt shoot through my veins. "Good evening, Aubrey…"

She dropped her glass to the floor and slowly turned around.

"*Andrew*?" She stepped back. "What are you doing here?"

"Does it matter?"

She didn't answer.

Neither of us said anything further, and that familiar tension that had always existed between us began to thicken with every second that passed.

She looked even more beautiful up close, and I was tempted to push her against the wall and reconnect, but I held back.

"Can I speak with you?" I asked.

She looked me up and down.

"Aubrey..." I looked into her eyes. "Can I speak with you?"

"No."

"Excuse me?" I raised my eyebrow.

"I said *no*." She crossed her arms. "As in, *no* you may not speak with me, and you can go back to wherever the hell you came from."

She walked away and headed to the dance floor.

I sighed and went after her, clasping her hand and spinning her around. "It'll only take five minutes."

"That's five more than I'm willing to give you."

"It's important."

"Are you *dying*?" Her face turned red. "Is it a life or death matter?"

"Does it really have to be?" My hand caressed her cheek, temporarily silencing her. "You look fucking beautiful tonight..."

"Thank you. My boyfriend thinks so, too."

"Your *boyfriend*?"

"Yes. You know, that person who doesn't treat you like shit just because he likes you and you like him back? Interesting concept, isn't it?"

I didn't get a chance to respond to that.

The orchestra struck a sudden loud chord that reverberated through the room, and a voice came over the speakers.

"Ladies and gentlemen," it said. "The Benjamin Wright Orchestra will now play their rendition of one of Tchaikovsky's most revered pieces. The tempo of this song has a similar pacing for what some of you may know as the waltz. Please join us on the floor for this classic homage..."

I grabbed her hand and entwined it with mine, securing my free hand around her waist.

"What are you doing?" She hissed and tried to pull away. "I'm not dancing with you."

I tightened my grip around her. "*Yes you are.*"

"Please don't make me scream, Andrew..."

"What makes you think I wouldn't love to hear that?"

She tried to move away from me, but I held her still.

"Five minutes," I said.

"*Three,*" she countered.

"Fine." I loosened my grip and swayed her to the music. "Are you aware that your boyfriend is a *male ballerina*?"

"The correct term," she said, rolling her eyes, "is a danseur."

"He's a fucking ballerina..." I dipped her to the floor. "Is this what you've been doing for the past few months?"

"Living out my dream free from a certain asshole?"

"I expect more from you if you're going to date someone else."

"I don't give a damn what you expect." She hissed. "He's everything you'll *never* be..."

"Because he kisses you in public?"

"It's more than that...But that's on the never-ending list of things he has on you."

"Does he make you cum?"

"He doesn't make me *cry.*"

Silence.

I felt her pulling away from me, but I held her still. "Are you fucking him?"

"Why do you care?"

"I don't. I just want to know."

"We haven't had a conversation in months and you think you're entitled to know who I'm sleeping with?"

"I wouldn't necessarily use the term *entitled*."

"No." She pressed her chest against mine. "No, I am not fucking him, but you know what? I will be soon."

"You have no reason to if I'm here."

She burst into laughter and stepped back. "You think I would sleep with you? Seriously?"

"Aubrey—"

"Do you really think I'm that stupid?" She cut me off. "I don't want anything to do with you, Andrew. You're nothing but a muse for an orgasm, a good visual for a hand-fuck, and I may miss you, but—"

"You miss me?"

"I miss the *idea* of you—of what you could've been."

"We can't be friends?"

"We can't be anything." Her lips were close to mine.

"Why am I finding that hard to believe?"

"You shouldn't." She glared at me. "Because in order for me to ever entertain you outside of this dance, I would have to take you back."

"Then take me back."

"*Please*!" She scoffed, looking angrier than I'd ever seen her before. "You would have to beg me to take you back, Andrew. Fucking *beg* me…"

"Hey Aubs." Her ballerina boyfriend interrupted us. "Is everything okay?"

"Yes." She stepped away from me and kissed his cheek. "Everything is more than okay."

"Who's your friend?"

"*No one*," she said. "Just some guy who made a donation."

"Thank you for your donation." He shook my hand like a woman and turned to Aubrey. "Are you ready to go home?"

"More than ready." She took his hand and walked away from me without glancing back.

———

I stood on the balcony of my hotel room, completely confused about what had happened a few hours ago. I was expecting Aubrey to leave with me, to come back to my hotel so we could fuck and catch up.

Unable to stop thinking about it, I sent her an email:

Subject: Your Address.
We need to finish our conversation. Tell me where you live so I can come over and talk.
—Andrew.

Subject: Re: Your Address.
I highly doubt you only want to talk. You just want to fuck. Nonetheless, I'm pretty sure Brian wouldn't appreciate you coming over tonight.
—Aubrey.

Subject: Re: Re: Your Address.
He's more than welcome to watch. He might actually learn something.
—Andrew.

No answer.

She didn't respond for a long time, and when she finally did, all she sent me was a text: "*Leave me alone, Andrew. Please.*"

I couldn't. I emailed her again.

Subject: Sponsor.
I bought golden level season tickets. One of the benefits is getting a tour from the cast-mate of my choice. It will definitely be you.
—Andrew.

Subject: Re: Sponsor.

Thank you for that pointless information. If you do choose me, we won't be alone, and I'll make sure that our tour ends in the exact time allotted.

Now, please leave me alone. I'm out with someone who admires my brain more than my pussy.

You had your chance, you fucked up, and I'm not sure why you're in New York right now but I really don't care. I seriously don't want to hear from you…Please go away.

—Aubrey

I sighed and scrolled down my contacts. I knew she was simply being difficult, and I wasn't going to let her get the last word. I pressed call on an old number and held it up to my ear.

"Who is this?" the old voice said over the line.

"I need an address."

"Who is this?"

"I need an address. Now."

"Liam?" There was a smile in his voice. "Is that you?"

"It's *Andrew*." I rolled my eyes. "Are you going to help me or not?"

"Well, since you asked so nicely…" There was a familiar humming sound in the background. "You know, I haven't heard from you since the last time I saw…" He stopped himself and cleared his throat. "What's the name?"

"Aubrey Everhart."

"Do you know what borough?"

"No," I said. "But the address can't be more than a few months old. She just moved here."

He was silent for a little while, tapping and touching buttons.

"Found it," he said. "7654 Fifth Avenue."

Five blocks away…

I thought about whether I should wait until morning to stop by, but I was already putting on my coat.

"It was nice hearing from you again, Liam..." the old man's voice brought me back to the present. "Good to know you're well and...getting over what happened."

"I'll never get over it." I hung up and headed outside, signaling for the town car driver to open the back door.

"Where to, Mr. Hamilton?" he asked.

"7654 Fifth Avenue."

"Right away."

It took less than twenty minutes to get there, and when we arrived I stared at the brownstone for a while. It looked like something I would've purchased years ago when I lived here, something far out of budget for a ballerina, so I figured her parents were paying the rent.

Stepping out of the car, I adjusted my coat and walked to her door—knocking five times.

"Coming!" She yelled.

The door swung open, but she wasn't standing behind it. It was her boyfriend.

"Um..." He looked confused. "Did you leave the pizza in your car or something?"

"I'm not a fucking pizza guy. Where is Aubrey?"

"It depends. Didn't we just see you at the gala?" He crossed his arms as Aubrey stepped into the doorway. "Who are you?"

"He's no one, *again*," she said, standing on her toes to kiss his lips.

He looked at me with his eyebrow raised as he returned her kiss.

"My cock has been in every inch of her mouth." I gritted my teeth.

Aubrey gasped, her cheeks turning bright red. "I am so sorry, Brian...Can you give us a moment please?"

He looked between the both of us, anger creeping onto his face, but he walked away.

"What do you fucking want, Andrew?" She fumed. "*What do you want*?"

"To talk."

"About *what*?"

"You and me, about us being friends again..."

"That will never fucking happen. Is that it?"

"Aubrey—"

"What brings you to New York, huh? Did you need to come back and fuck some familiar women on Date-Match? Did Durham somehow run out of pussy?"

"It's actually starting to feel that way."

She started to close the door, but I held it still with my hand.

"I miss you, Aubrey..." I looked directly into her eyes. "I really do, and I'm...I'm sorry for kicking you out that night."

"You should be." Her voice was a whisper. "And if you really miss me, you'll leave me alone."

"Why would I do that?"

"Because you're bipolar. Because the second I ask one too many questions, or suggest something outside of your comfort zone, you'll treat me like trash again and I'd rather cut my losses now." She wiped a tear from her eyes. "I was your only friend—your only fucking friend, and you treated me worse than any of the women you met online. If anything, *I'm* sorry that I ever let you do that. Please leave."

"Aubrey, listen..."

"Is there super glue on my floor?" She pushed me down a step. "Is that why you're still standing there?"

"Please, just—"

"Lie about one thing, lie about it all, right?" She pushed me again. "You're still the biggest liar between the two of us. Lying by omission is still lying."

"Can you please calm down and let me talk about this with you inside?"

"I thought you hated rhetorical questions." She slammed the door in my face.

a priori assumption (n.):

An assumption that is true without further proof or need to prove it.

Aubrey

I woke up the next morning on edge, in utter shock.

I couldn't believe Andrew was in New York, couldn't believe he'd admitted missing me on my front steps last night.

Seeing him again brought out every emotion in me, and even though I'd told Brian that Andrew and I were done, I'd spent the rest of our date last night thinking about him.

Him and his perfect suit. Him and his perfect lips that nearly pressed against mine as we argued. And, shamefully, him and his perfect cock that I felt hardening in his pants as he dipped me on the dance floor.

Ugh!

I got out of bed and sent Brian a text. "Today is my one on one day with Ashcroft…Wish me luck!"

His response came immediately. "Good luck, babe! Get some coffee, you're going to need it…"

Slipping into the shower, I scolded myself. "Brian is a sweetheart and he's good for you…He may suck at phone sex, and you may have no desire to sleep with him right now, but he treats you better than you've ever been treated before…"

When I was wrinkled and prune-like, I stepped out and checked the time.

4:30 a.m.

I had twenty minutes to make it to the closest subway station and avoid the ire of Ashcroft. Throwing on some old sweatpants, I grabbed my ballet bag and snatched my coat from the bannister in the hallway. I double checked my wallet to make sure I had my metro pass, and when I opened the door, I found myself face to face with a stranger and a cup of steaming hot coffee.

"Good luck at practice today," he said, handing it over. "This was made especially for you."

"Since when do coffee shops deliver?"

He shrugged. "They don't."

I stared at the cup as he walked away, noticing that my name was etched atop the whipped cream in thin caramel, and that "Good luck," was written in cursive on the label.

It was a signature, sweet Brian move, and I immediately felt guilty for not giving him my full attention last night. As I walked to the subway, sipping what was arguably the best coffee I'd ever had, I vowed to give him my full attention from here on out.

I deleted all of Andrew's old texts and emails, even the ones I'd fake deleted by placing them in the archive. I blocked his number, preventing his calls from ever getting through, and although I couldn't block his emails, I changed the settings of my inbox so they would go straight to my spam folder.

When I finally arrived at practice that morning, I danced better than I'd ever danced before…

———

Later that night...

"How do you find the time to take the subway just to meet me at practice and walk me home?" I looked up at Brian as we crossed the street. "Where do you find the energy?"

"I make time for all the things I really like." He kissed my forehead.

"Do you want to catch a movie this weekend? My treat? I owe you one..."

"What makes you say that?"

"I still feel bad about gala night and what that guy from my past said to you," I said. "I'm really sorry."

"No worries. I'm sure he's—" He stopped talking as we approached my house, pointing at the man who was leaning against the door.

Andrew.

I took a deep breath as Andrew walked down the steps.

"Good evening, Aubrey," he said, smirking. "And your name is *danseur*, correct?"

"It's *Brian*."

"Close enough."

Brian crossed his arms. "I could've sworn I overheard her say that she didn't want you anymore. Why can't you take the hint?"

"Because she says things she doesn't mean all the time." He looked at me, instantly setting my nerves on fire. "And I know she's just angry with me."

"Dude!" Brian let out an exasperated sigh. "I'm her boyfriend so clearly she's moved on...She has a *boyfriend*."

"I honestly don't feel threatened," he said, still looking at me. "Did you get my coffee this morning?"

What?! "That was from you?" My eyes widened. "I thought..."

"What coffee, Aubs?" Brian looked concerned. "What is he talking about?"

"Andrew…" I shook my head. "Thank you for the coffee, but that doesn't make up for anything…"

"I never said it did."

A cold wind brushed by and I felt myself being drawn to him, literally drawn to him, and I took a few steps forward. But then I took a few steps back.

"I'm with Brian now…" I grabbed Brian's hand and led him up to my door, refusing to look back at a seemingly hurt Andrew.

I shut the door and peeped through my blinds, noticing that he was still standing there. Confused.

"Look, Aubs…" The sound of Brian's voice got my attention. "I don't think the two of us are going to work."

"*What*? No, no, no. Of course, we will. This is just a minor issue."

"I think your heart and mind are elsewhere…I think they always have been, actually."

"Seriously?" I crossed my arms. "Because some psycho from my past shows up for one night and suddenly wants me again? That's what makes you think that?"

"That, and the fact that some psycho sent me a text earlier today that said, "Her pussy belongs to me." I'm just now remembering that…"

I sighed and he walked over, kissing my forehead.

"If it's a minor issue, and he doesn't mean anything to you anymore, we can try again in a month."

"A month?"

He nodded. "That way I'll know for sure, and our phone sex will be twice as amazing since we won't have had it in so long… Then, maybe we can upgrade to actual sex."

I said nothing, and he walked out of my place.

I peeped through the blinds again, watching him disappear into the night, and then I noticed that Andrew was still standing outside.

Livid, I stomped down the steps and headed straight toward him. "Do you have any idea how much I hate you right now?"

"Hate isn't something that can be adequately measured."

"You just ruined the one great relationship I had in this city. You just made him dump me."

"Good," he said. "I did you a favor."

"Is this how you're planning on getting me to talk to you again?"

"Part of it."

"It's not going to work." I pressed my finger against his chest, emphasizing every syllable. "I told you that you would have to fucking beg me, and since I know that's not how you operate—"

"You don't know how I fucking operate."

"Are you going to walk me to the subway station every morning?"

"I have a fucking car."

"Walk me back from rehearsals?"

"Same answer."

"Actually treat me with some goddamn respect?"

He cupped my face in his hands. "If you give me a chance to..."

I stepped back, still angry. "I'm not holding my breath."

omission (n.):

Inadvertently leaving out a word, phrase or other language from a contract, deed, judgment or other document.

Aubrey

Subject: Brian-gate.
I'm not sure how many more times I'll have to apologize for making your "boyfriend" dump you, but I am, in fact, sorry. Then again, maybe I should have waited until after you fucked him so you could be more appreciative.
—Andrew

"Ugh!" I tossed my phone across the room, nearly knocking over the beautiful vase of lilies he sent me yesterday.

Ever since last week's "Brian-gate," I had to face him every day in some capacity. In the mornings, he personally brought me my favorite coffee, walked me to the block where my subway stop was, and apologized profusely. In his own way, of course.

I never said a word back, though. I just sipped from my cup and listened.

Taking a seat on my couch, I grabbed an ice wrap and placed it on my shoulders. I was counting down the days to opening night, wondering how much more pain my body could take.

My feet were now unrecognizable; I no longer soothed their cuts and blisters. The muscles in my arms ached relentlessly, and when I told Mr. Ashcroft that I needed a few extra minutes to stretch my right leg yesterday, he said, "Then I need to replace you with a dancer who doesn't."

I cringed at the memory and heard a knock at my door.

"Coming!" I walked over and opened it, tempted to slam it shut once I saw Andrew.

"Yes?" I asked.

"Practice starts in an hour. You're going to be late."

"I'm not due there until the afternoon session. Thank you for the reminder."

"Can I come in until then?"

"No."

"Why not?"

"Do I really need a reason?"

"I just want to talk to you for a few minutes, Aubrey."

"We can do that over the phone."

"You blocked my fucking number." He narrowed his eyes at me. "I've tried that already today. Twice."

"Have you tried email?"

"Aubrey, please…" He actually looked sincere.

"Fine." I held the door open. "But you have to leave in five minutes so I can take a nap."

He stepped inside and looked around, running his hands over the artwork in the halls.

Looking slightly impressed, he rubbed his chin. "Are your parents paying for this?"

"No, I haven't spoken to them since I left." I admitted. "A retired dancer from the company rents out all her condos to the newest cohorts."

"Is it expensive?"

"Not at all." I sat on the couch. "It's the only way I can afford to live in this part of town. Otherwise, I'd be sleeping in a cardboard box."

He stared at me for a while, not saying a word.

"What is it?" I asked.

"Nothing. It's just been awhile since you spoke a full sentence that wasn't filled with malice."

"Don't get used to it." I winced and placed another ice wrap on my shoulder. "I'm just trying to make your five minutes with me somewhat memorable."

"They will be."

Silence.

He walked over and sat next to me on the couch. "You got an A on your final assignment at GBH."

"Did you give it to me out of sympathy?"

"I gave it to you because your work was the best." He looked into my eyes. "Although, I could have done without the "FYI: Mr. Hamilton used to fuck me in his office" note that was at the end."

I held back a laugh.

"Jessica misses you by the way."

"Really?"

"She claims I was much more desirable when you were around," he said. "And apparently she used to listen to us have sex."

"What?"

"There's no point in even trying to fire her anymore…I think she grew on me."

"Do all the interns still hate you?"

"No." He smiled. "For some strange reason, they started to like me shortly after you left."

"Are you insinuating that your asshole behavior was my fault?"

"No." He pulled me into his lap and took the ice wrap away. "I'm insinuating that I no longer pretend to care about any interns when my favorite one is missing."

I blushed and he started to massage my shoulders—slowly kneading his hands against my skin.

I shut my eyes and exhaled, slightly tilting my head back instead of telling him to stop.

"Do you plan on ever accepting my apology?" he asked, pressing a kiss against my neck.

"No."

"Is there any way that I could *make you*?" His fingers gently rubbed my collarbone, alleviating the pain.

"You could tell me the real reason you're in New York…" I felt him unsnapping my bra. "I know you didn't come all the way here just to see me."

He kissed my shoulder. "You *don't* know that."

"I'm serious, Andrew."

"As am I." He pressed his palms into my back, temporarily rendering me speechless. "You're a huge part of the reason why I'm still here, actually."

"And the other part?"

He tilted my head back so I was looking directly into his eyes. "The other part doesn't really matter." He looked as if he wanted to kiss me, but he held back.

Instead, he slipped his hands underneath my legs and flipped me over so I was lying in his lap. "What time is your rehearsal again?"

"Four…" I barely managed. His touches felt too good.

"Can I drive you?" He softly kneaded the back of my shoulders. "I can do this to you for longer if you don't take the subway…"

I nodded and shut my eyes, falling asleep at the mercy of his hands.

Hours later, Andrew pulled over to the curb at Lincoln Center.

I unbuckled my seatbelt and looked at him. "Are you going to be standing outside the ballet hall when I get done today?"

"Probably."

"With hot chocolate?"

"Would you prefer something different?"

I smiled. "No…"

He leaned over and tucked a strand of hair behind my ear. "I thought I was doing the right thing by kicking you out that night, by pushing you away…It was definitely a mistake."

"I'm not coming back to you just because you said that."

"I didn't ask you to." He trailed his finger against my lips. "I would, however, like you to consider forgiving me."

"I'll think about it. Just because you—"

His lips were on mine—kissing me, begging me, saying all the things he couldn't say with words. And this time I was listening, missing everything we once had before he pushed me away.

Not letting me go, he ran his fingers through my hair and caressed my neck.

"Go think about *that*," he whispered, slowly pulling away from me.

"Um…" I struggled to catch my breath as he stepped out to open my door.

"I'll see you tonight." He kissed my lips before leaving me standing in the middle of the street, completely breathless again.

Shit…

I headed toward the dance hall, confident that I would dance like I was on air today. I opened the doors and felt someone grabbing my shoulder from behind.

"Aubrey?" The voice asked. "Aubrey, is that you?"

I turned around, shocked. "*Mom*? What are you doing here?"

"I wanted to see you…"

I noticed the pin on her suit, "Vote Smart. Vote Everhart," and knew that wasn't true. She was in town for something that had to do with my father's campaign; I was only a pit stop.

"Well, now you've seen me…" I turned away and slipped inside the building.

"Wait, Aubrey." She followed me. "Do you really think that moving across the country was the best way to get me and your father's attention?"

"I didn't leave North Carolina to get your attention."

"Well, you certainly have it."

"And look, it only took twenty two years…"

She sighed. "We've decided to talk to the department chair about letting you pick up where you left off during the summer semester. We can do that since you're so upset about being a part of the campaign."

"I'm not upset. I honestly don't care."

"Of course you do." She sounded offended. "But if it makes you feel any better, we placed a picture of you and one of your ballets in our campaign brochure."

"Did you do that so you could look like you actually care about college arts?"

"No, we donated fifty thousand dollars to Duke's dance program to look like we actually care about college arts. The brochure picture was *personal*, although it would've been even better if you wrote that essay we begged you to write. We could've put that next to the picture. "

I felt a pang in my chest. "When does your flight leave, mother?"

"Excuse me?"

"When does your flight leave?" I repeated, my voice cracking. "I'm pretty sure it's in three hours or less so you won't have to spend a full day here, so you can go back and tell Dad that you tried to convince me to come home after you fulfilled your campaign work. I'm sure that's still all that matters to you."

She was silent.

"I left Durham because I'll be living here for at least three years—which is the length of my contract with the company, where I'll be pursuing my real dream. And I must say, it's just a bonus that I won't be anywhere near you."

She gasped.

"Have a safe flight. Tell Dad I said hello."

"You're just going to leave me standing here?"

"You've done it to me my entire life." I left the building. I was too angry, too hurt, to completely focus.

I sent Ashcroft an email—letting him know I was using a sick day, and headed for the street.

"Aubrey!" My mother called from behind, but I kept walking. "Aubrey, wait!"

She finally caught up to me and grabbed my arm. "I can miss my flight…"

"And why would you want to do that?"

"So I can spend time with my daughter before she forgets that I exist…"

I held back tears.

"I can stay here for a few days and we can catch up in between your dance schedule," she said. "I'll make your dad fly up too if that's okay with you?"

"That would be perfectly fine…" I nodded, but then it hit me. "No campaign talk, though."

"Done deal."

"No talking about me going back to law school, either."

"I can live with that, too." She nodded.

"And no talking shit about ballet."

She hesitated, but she nodded again. "Okay, fine." She hugged me. "Can you hail us a cab so I can book a room at the Four Seasons?"

"Why? You can just stay at my place."

"Oh, please." She slid a pair of shades over her eyes. "I looked up what professional ballerinas make. I know what type of apartment you can afford in this city, and daughter or not, I refuse."

I didn't want to laugh, but I couldn't help it. I knew making up would be a long process, but I was willing to give it a try.

She walked over to a newspaper stand, and I held out my hand for a cab.

"Oh, *The New York Times* always picks the best cases to cover." She flipped through the paper. "There's one hell of a trial going on this week."

"Criminal or corporate?" I asked as a taxi flew right past me.

"Both," she said. "And I actually know this guy. Well, I know *of* him anyway...Absolutely incredible lawyer..."

"We're never going to get a cab at this rate." I shook my head at being snubbed again.

"I doubt he'll ever get recognition for that government case..."

"What are you talking about?"

"Liam Henderson." She held the paper in front of me, pointing to a picture-less article. "Remember? He's on me and your dad's list of lawyers who'll never be given the credit they deserve because they went against the government. This guy was your favorite, I do believe."

"Oh, yeah." I remembered. "So, why is he in the paper now? Did he mess up because he didn't receive his due fame? Is he in trouble?"

"No, looks like he's just testifying in a case. Article claims he's been living down in the South and even partnered at some firm, but that can't be true. Any firm down there would be bragging if they had him, and I haven't heard anything."

"I'm sure they would." I finally waved down a cab. "We can go now."

"It's quite weird though." She tapped her lip. "In all of his career, I've never seen a picture of him—maybe one or two, but they were stock pictures from his college days. I'm sure he looks different now."

"Mom," I said, opening the car door. "The cab charges by the minute."

"Now the article claims he's been living in North Carolina under an assumed name for the past six years. But of course, they're not revealing *that* name. They need to get better researchers, don't you think? How could a lawyer of that status manage to change his name, switch states, and still practice the law?" She handed me the paper as she stepped into the cab. "He'd have to erase his entire identity and start all over. Who would do that?"

I gasped and flipped to the article as I sat in the backseat. I read it word for word, over and over, and everything around me became a blur. I could practically feel my jaw dropping as I flashed back to my first interview at GBH:

Miss Everhart, are there any lawyers that you wish to model your own career after?" Mr. Bach smiled at me.

"Yes, actually," I said. "I've always admired the career of Liam Henderson."

"Liam Henderson?" Andrew looked up at me with his eyebrow raised. "Who is that?"

suppression of evidence (n.):

The improper hiding of evidence by a prosecutor who is constitutionally required to reveal to the defense all evidence.

Andrew

Former Partners to Finally Appear in Court Opposite Each Other: Hart Case Continues This Week.

That's what the headline in the judicial section of *The New York Times* read this morning. To those who knew nothing about the case, I was sure that it was simply another story to pass the time, another superficial scandal to devour with their morning breakfast.

But for me, it was the end of a six year chapter that had gone on for far too many pages. It was part of the reason why I left, part of the reason why after I testified in a few days, I would leave this city for the very last time.

I looked outside the window at the Waldorf Astoria's restaurant, wondering how it could possibly be raining so heavily in the dead of winter.

"Mr. Hamilton?" A woman in a suit stepped next to my table.

"Yes?"

"I'm Vera Milton, the general manager," she said. "You've had several calls from a Miss Ava Sanchez…She keeps telling us that it's important and that she needs to speak with you. She's on the line for you now…"

I sighed. "Could you patch her call to my room in two minutes please?"

"Certainly sir."

I left the newspaper on the table and headed straight for the penthouse suite. As soon as I unlocked the door, the phone in the parlor room rang.

"Hello?" I answered.

"It's me…" Ava said softly.

"I'm aware. How did you find out where I was staying?"

"Really?" She scoffed. "I need you to do me a favor…"

"Goodbye, Ava."

"No, wait." She sounded frantic. "I really am sorry for everything I did to you, Liam."

"What did I tell you about calling me that?"

"I remember when you visited me when I was being held in jail—before all the hearings started…Remember?" She paused. "I know how hard seeing me must have been back then, how lonely you had to be to come and visit *me* of all people…You even told me you were contemplating changing your name to Andrew and leaving New York…And then I begged you to save me. Remember that?"

"I'm really not in the mood for story time right now."

"You were such a softie back then…So compassionate, so caring—"

"Get to the fucking point, Ava."

"At the trial this week, I know that Kevin—"

"I.e. my former best friend that you fucked?"

"Yes." She sighed. "Him…"

"What about him?"

"He's not the monster you think he is."

"Are you calling about a favor that's never going to happen, or are you calling to be his fucking character witness? I'm confused."

"He's still sorry for what he did…He was—"

"Which one is it, Ava?" I snapped. "I'm not a fan of this vague shit."

"Do you really want to hurt him?" Her voice softened. "I think you've already punished us enough. I'm already behind bars, so there's really no need for him to suffer at this point. "

"The two of you will never suffer enough." I hung up and sent a text to an old contact I had at corrections, telling him that Ava had contraband in her cell.

The last thing I wanted to think about was my old partner and former best friend. The only time he needed to be thought of was during the upcoming hearing, and never again after that.

I scrolled through my text messages, noticing that Aubrey had sent me a simple "Okay" when I asked how today's audition went.

With the exception of the day I massaged her shoulders, she was still being short with me.

I opened my inbox to send her a longer message, but I saw that she'd sent me one first.

Subject: Yes.
I just received your newest set of flowers and your note about going on a date tonight…I have a few stipulations, though.
—Aubrey

Subject: Re: Yes.
Name them.
—Andrew

She sent a new message.

Subject: Date.
I'm allowed to ask you whatever I want and you have to answer truthfully.
—Aubrey

Subject: Re: Date.
I always answer truthfully. Is the word "stipulations" not plural?
—Andrew

Subject: Re: Re: Date.
You have to be a complete gentleman. I don't want to be fucked in another bathroom…
What time are you picking me up?
—Aubrey

Subject: Re: Re: Re: Date.
I actually wasn't planning on fucking you tonight, but since you've clearly entertained that possibility, I'll be sure to send a list of potential locations prior to the date.
Eight o' clock.
—Andrew

I knocked on her door at 7:58, dressed in a black designer suit I'd purchased hours ago.

There was no answer, and before I could knock again, the door swung open and she stepped out wearing a short black dress that left little to the imagination.

"Are you aware that it's still winter?" I trailed my finger along her exposed shoulders. "You're going to need a coat."

She looked behind me. "You took the subway here?"

"Yes."

"We're taking the subway on our *date*?"

"The car will come later." I smiled as confusion spread across her face.

She grabbed her coat from inside and shut the door, looking up at me. "Do you even know how to use the subway?"

"Of course I do," I said, clasping her hand. "I wasn't always well-off when I lived here..."

A light snow fell as we made our way to the subway tunnel, and she leaned against me—pressing her body closer to mine. Holiday lights were strung about the tallest buildings—sparkling against the night, and a faint sense of excitement swirled through the air.

There weren't that many people out tonight, and as we boarded a nearly empty train, Aubrey laughed at that fact.

"This is the first time I've ever seen a subway like this," she said. "I usually have to fight for my own tiny space."

"Hmmm." I prevented her from taking a seat, instead making her share a pole with me. "How did your audition really go today? Surely you have more to say about it than okay."

"I was crying when I sent that text. I was overwhelmed."

I raised my eyebrow.

"I landed Odette/Odile in *Swan Lake*—on a *professional* level." She looked as if she was about to burst into tears. "I still can't believe it...All of my dreams are actually coming true."

"Maybe you're meant to play that role..." I wiped a stray tear from her eyes.

"Maybe." She leaned closer. "I'm just happy that they're giving us the next few days off...I think I'll be able to relax and keep up with the news a bit more. You know, actually have some semblance of a life outside of the dance hall."

"You could spend more time with me if you want to take a break. The news in this city is overrated and mostly false."

"Is that so?"

"Yes," I said, looking into her eyes. "I wouldn't believe half of the shit in any of these papers."

She smiled. "Have you heard anything about the huge trial that's happening this week?"

"I'm pretty sure there's more than one."

"No…" She shook her head. "Not like this one…"

I hesitated. "What makes this one so special?"

"It's more intriguing than special…It's about two lawyers who once shared a firm—both of them were big shots, you know? One of them even won against the government in his very first case."

"It was probably a lucky break."

"I don't think so." She looked into my eyes. "I've read the transcripts. He knew exactly what he was doing, and the verdict actually affected public policy."

I said nothing.

"But the thing is, he never got credit for his work—outside of word of mouth from people who knew the details, you know?" She paused. "But anyway, from what I've read and pieced together, it seems like he was falsely accused of a laundry list of federal charges a few years later."

"*Aubrey…*"

"It looks like everyone ran with the story—all of the papers, all of the news outlets, and the truth wasn't filtered until months later, after his name was already tarnished."

I stared at her, begging her to stop, but she continued.

"The charges are still pending against his old partner to this day, that's just how many there were. But *him*—this upstanding lawyer with one hell of a track record, he just vanished. Into thin air."

"If he was that upstanding, then I'm pretty sure that's impossible."

"Is it?"

"*It is*," I said.

"I thought that, too…" She searched my eyes for answers. "But I think the guy I'm talking about is capable of anything."

"What are the names in this case you're speaking of?"

"The accused is Kevin Hart, and the key witness is Liam Henderson."

"I'll google it tonight." I sighed, not wanting to continue this conversation.

A voice came over the speakers, announcing our stop, and I took her hand again.

"I know you made me agree to stipulations," I said, looking at her as we stepped off, "but can you agree to one of mine?"

"Depends on what it is."

"Ask me the deep conversation questions after dinner."

"Is that where we're going right now?"

"No." I led her up the steps. "I wouldn't dare. I don't want you accusing me of treating you like all my other dates."

"Does that mean you won't fuck me at the end?"

"It means I won't leave you at the end."

She blushed, and I kissed her forehead as we walked through the streets of flashing lights and sparkling billboards.

She didn't say much of anything else as we moved from block to block, only blushing each time I looked at her.

"Here," I said, stopping her as we approached our first destination.

"Broadway?" She looked up at the grand marquis.

"You mentioned you haven't had the chance to come here yet," I said. "I used to come here all the time when I lived here…"

"All the time?"

"At least once a week." I held the door open for her. "Twice when this particular play was performed." I ran my fingers across the words, *Death of a Salesman*, before handing our tickets to the usher.

She smiled as he led us to the private balcony, as he offered us complimentary wine since we were so early.

"I would've never taken you for the drama type," she said, taking a sip from her glass. "You've never mentioned that to me before."

"I actually almost went to theater school instead of law school."

"What made you change your mind?"

"A law degree attracts a higher percentage of pussy."

"What?!" She rolled her eyes, laughing. "I'm being serious."

"I received a bigger scholarship for law school." I resisted the urge to pull her into my lap. "Best decision I ever made."

She opened her mouth to respond, but the lights began to dim and she leaned closer to me, whispering, "I would've liked to see you as an actor…I think you would've been really good at it."

I felt her placing her hand on my thigh. "I don't think I would've wanted to see you play anything serious though. I think I would prefer—"

"Are you going to talk through this entire play, Aubrey?" I cut her off, ignoring the tell-tale look on her face—the one of severe longing, needing.

"Am I not allowed to make comments?" She sounded offended. "Am I not allowed to do that until *after dinner* either? If that's the case, why even take me out? Why would you even—"

"I've seen this play a million times…" I pressed my finger against her lips as the lead actor stepped onto the stage. "And although I want you to experience it too, if you would rather me entertain you in a *different* way, just tell me."

"What?"

"Would this balcony make it onto your list of approved places?" I asked. "If I fucked you here, would that still count as me being a gentleman?"

Her eyes widened and she quickly moved her hand away from my lap. “I was just teasing you, Andrew…”

“I’m aware.” I kissed her neck. “And I’ve told you on numerous occasions that I don’t appreciate that, whether you’re mad at me or not…”

She sucked in a breath as I slid my thumb underneath her panties.

“I’ll stop asking questions,” she said. “I’ll watch the play…”

As she turned her face toward the stage, I moved out of my seat and kneeled in front of her.

“Andrew?” She whispered harshly as I spread her thighs apart. “What are you doing?”

“Making sure you enjoy the show.”

I didn’t give her a chance to respond. I quickly ripped off her panties, and buried my head in between her legs, running my tongue against her bare pussy—enjoying a taste I’d missed for months. I sucked her clit between my lips, shutting my eyes as it swelled in my mouth.

“Andrew….” She moaned as she squeezed her legs around my neck, grabbing onto my hair and begging me to slow down.

I couldn’t. She tasted too fucking good.

I forced my tongue deeper inside of her, claiming every part, marking what was mine.

Her hips began to rise off the seat, and I pushed them down—punishing her with stronger strokes, slipping my fingers inside of her and commanding her to stay still.

“I can’t…” She thrust her hips up again. “I can’t…”

A loud applause arose from the theater below us, echoing off the walls as the first scene ended.

I sucked her clit harder, darting my tongue against it repeatedly until she couldn’t help but scream my name across the theater.

Shaking, she grabbed my shoulders, gripping me harder than ever as she came into my mouth.

I held her thighs as she continued to shake, as tremor after tremor ran through her body.

As she came back down, I caressed her legs and kissed the inside of her thighs.

Grabbing her ripped panties off the floor, I wiped her clean. Then I stuffed them into my pocket before taking my seat again.

"Is something wrong sir?" An usher stepped into our balcony. "I heard a disturbance."

"A *disturbance*?" I looked at Aubrey then back at him. "No, I don't think there was one here."

"Are you sure?" he asked concerned. "What about you, Miss? Are you okay?"

"Yes sir." Aubrey nodded, attempting to look as normal as possible. "I'm more than fine."

He walked away, and within seconds, she seemingly transformed into the Aubrey I remembered from months ago, the one that was incapable of not asking questions.

Not that I minded, though.

By the first intermission she'd asked all that was possible about the play and leaned against me, whispering, "This is perfect, Andrew…Thank you." And then she didn't speak again until the show ended two hours later.

"The lead was amazing," she said as the curtains closed. "I really felt all of his emotions in that last scene…"

"Me too." I helped her into her coat. "Do you have a curfew? Any time that I need to get you back home?"

"I'm twenty two years old."

"I'm well aware." I rolled my eyes. "I found that out the hard way, thank you. I meant, do you have a few more hours to spend with me or do you have to get up early?"

"Not until the afternoon…"

"Good." I led her out of the theater and signaled to the town-car driver across the street. "I want to take you somewhere else. Can I?"

"I would love that..."

I helped her into the town car and after I slid inside, she moved into my lap—pressing her lips against mine, whispering thanks once again.

Holding her close, I gave her a brief tour of my past as we drove through the city—grateful that the driver avoided driving by my former firm.

I showed her my favorite restaurants, my favorite places to relax, and a few places I would like to take her to before I left.

"We've arrived at the Waldorf Astoria, Mr. Hamilton." The driver looked at us through the rearview mirror. "Will this be the final stop for the night?"

"Yes," I said, noticing Aubrey narrowing her eyes at me.

"I thought you said—"

"Relax..." I kissed her forehead. "This is where I've been living since I flew here."

"Oh..."

I took her hand and walked her through the lobby and onto the elevator that led to the roof.

Opening the doors, I noticed everything was set up exactly as I asked: A lone white clothed table sat in front of a dancing fire, soft lights hung in waves across the trellis, and through the falling snow, the words "I'm sorry" twinkled against the building directly across from us.

"This is so beautiful, Andrew..." she said, looking around. "When did you change your mind about dinner?"

"I didn't." I pulled out her chair and uncovered the platter of chocolate and vanilla covered strawberries. "It's dessert."

"Did you think of all this yourself?"

"I did." I sat next to her and put my arms around her shoulders.

"You know," she said, "typically on a date the two people sit across from each other."

"Did you miss the memo about me making sure that I wouldn't treat you like any other date?"

"Not at all." Her mouth was on mine within seconds and my hands found their way into her hair.

Pulling her forward, I bit her lips and looked into her eyes.

She was silently telling me to take things further, rubbing her hand against my cock.

"Stop touching me, Aubrey," I whispered, warning her. "I'm not going to be able to be a gentleman anymore if you don't stop..." I stood up and walked to the door, giving myself some space. "I'm trying to prove to you that I can get through a date without fucking you..."

She followed me, smiling. "I'm pretty sure you already failed at that..." She threaded her fingers through my hair and hastily unbuttoned my shirt.

I wedged my knee between her legs and slid a hand across her thighs, sighing as I felt how wet she was.

"Aubrey..." I groaned as she reached into my pocket and pulled out a condom. "I can wait..."

"I can't." She freed my cock from my pants and rolled the condom onto me without letting my lips go.

I secured my arms around her waist and lifting her up, carrying her over to the rooftop's railing. "You have no idea how much I've missed your pussy." I kissed her lips. "And your mouth."

"Is that all you miss?" Her hands went around my neck.

"If it was, then we wouldn't be here right now." I slowly slid inside of her, filling her inch by inch, staring into her eyes as I remembered just how good she fucking felt.

Without saying another word, I slid my hands down to her sides and moved her up and down—groaning as her pussy gripped me tighter and tighter with every stroke.

Her lips found their way to mine, and neither of us let go—grinding into each other as a second light snow fell over us.

Her nails dug into my back as she came close to coming, her teeth trapped my bottom lip to prevent herself from screaming out.

"Don't let go yet, Aubrey…" My cock was throbbing inside of her. "Wait…"

She shook her head, fighting it, but she held on for a few more seconds—looking into my eyes.

"I missed you so much," I whispered. "So fucking much…"

Falling forward into my chest, she came with me—biting my skin as her legs went limp around my waist.

Both of us were breathing heavily, staring at each other as we once did months ago, and we remained entwined.

I kissed her lips, repeating how much I missed her, and she smiled—softly telling me to pull out of her.

"Would you like to stay the night?" I asked, picking up my jacket and holding it out for her. "You can tell me more about that case you're so intrigued with lately."

"The Henderson & Hart one?" she asked. "You really haven't heard anything about it?"

"No, but if you spend the night we can google it together."

"I don't think so." Her voice was suddenly flat. "I need to go." She adjusted her dress and walked over to the table, picking up her purse. '

"Is something wrong?"

She didn't answer. She pulled out her phone to check the time and sighed.

"Aubrey, what are you doing?"

"Forcing myself to see that you're still the same and you'll never change." She looked hurt. "Your idea of the truth is, and will always be, duplicitous. That's all."

"Excuse me?"

"Thank you for a wonderful night…I'll always remember this and cherish it, just so you know."

"I'm really starting to wonder if you are, indeed, *bipolar*…"

"Why didn't you tell me that your name was Liam Henderson tonight?" She shook her head, and I inhaled a sharp breath.

"I gave you every opportunity to," she said, looking hurt. "I practically begged you to tell me, but you opened up about everything except for that."

I hesitated. "I was going to tell you everything later tonight, in bed."

"Sure you were." She scoffed. "Is there any reason why you didn't even tell me this when I said you were once my favorite lawyer in my interview?"

"Once?"

She nodded. "Yes. *Once.* The essays I used to read by Liam all stressed complete and utter honesty. I guess that all changed once he became *Andrew*."

"Aubrey, don't…" I stepped forward and she took a step back. "I was honestly going to ask you to come to the final hearing."

"Can I use your town car to get home or do I need to call a cab?"

"Stop this. Now."

"Cab it is." She shrugged. "I wish you the best of luck with your testimony. And I hope you treat the next girl you find nicely from the beginning so she won't have to love and leave you alone in the end."

"Give me a chance to talk, Aubrey…"

"We have nothing more to discuss." She opened the door. "*Please* do not follow me, Andrew. You can't trust me and I can't trust you, so I don't want anything to do with this anymore and I need you to finally respect that."

I opened my mouth to respond, but she spoke first.

"Goodbye Andrew, *Liam*," she said, "whatever the hell your name is."

"Aubrey…"

The door slammed shut and I knew it was pointless to go after her in that moment.

She was gone.

swear (v.):

To declare under oath that one will tell the truth.

Andrew

"Do you swear to tell the truth, the whole truth, and nothing but the truth so help you God?" The judge said to me a few mornings later.

I said nothing, the sudden departure of Aubrey still fresh on my mind.

"Mr. Hamilton, I asked you a question." The judge chided.

"I apologize," I said. "I do swear to tell the truth, the whole truth, and nothing but the truth so help me God."

"We may proceed."

The defense lawyer stood up and cleared his throat. "Mr. Hamilton, your legal name was formerly Liam Henderson, correct?"

"Correct."

"Could you please tell the court how you know my client, Kevin Hart?"

"We were once partners at Henderson & Hart."

"Partners *and* best friends, correct?"

I looked over at an expressionless Kevin. He was dressed in a grey suit, still incapable of wearing a matching tie.

"Yes," I said to the lawyer. "Once upon a time."

"Is it true that you got into an altercation with him at a bar six and a half years ago?"

"Define altercation."

He picked up a sheet of paper. "Did you walk into a bar and punch him? Leaving him with a broken jaw and a fractured ribcage?"

"He was fucking my wife."

The jurors gasped and the judge banged his gavel.

"*Mr. Hamilton...*" The judge spoke sternly. "That type of language is not allowed in my courtroom. Please answer the question."

"Yes," I said. "Yes, I did injure Mr. Hart...*Severely*."

"Similarly to how you injured your own wife?"

"*Objection*!" The prosecutor stood up. "Relevance, Your Honor?"

"Sustained."

"Fine." The defense lawyer held up his hands in surrender. "Is it true that you blame Mr. Hart for the downfall of your former firm?"

"Clearly the Department of Justice does since he's the one on trial today."

"*Mr. Hamilton...*"

"Yes." I clenched my jaw. "Yes, I blame him for the demise of our former firm."

"Is it true that you also blame him for the unfortunate death of your daughter?"

"*Your Honor*!" The prosecutor shot me a look of sympathy. "Relevance?"

"Overruled...Answer the question, Mr. Hamilton."

I looked away from Kevin and balled my fists. "Yes."

"Your daughter died amidst the weeks leading up to the complete collapse of your firm, and within those weeks you managed to severely beat your partner, batter your wife—"

"I didn't batter my fucking wife. She made that shit up. Have you done any fucking research?"

The judge banged his gavel, but I continued talking.

"I'm not sure what low level community college was dumb enough to issue you a law degree, but the case between me and my wife was thrown out years ago because she lied about numerous things to a grand jury. And seeing as though she was sent to prison and I was cleared of all charges, you can accept that as a fucking fact. So, before you ask me another bullshit question and try to damage my character, remember that *your* client's livelihood is at stake during this trial. Not mine."

The judge let out a deep sigh, but he didn't say anything further. He just motioned for the defense to continue.

"During your partnership, is it true that your wife was in charge of all the firm's monetary dealings?"

"Ex-wife. And yes."

"And you never thought to double check where she was allocating most of the funds?"

"I had a degree in law, not accounting."

"So, you never thought it was slightly suspicious that your new firm was bringing in seven figures monthly?"

"No." I sighed, thinking back to those days, those clients. Everyone we dealt with had far more than I would earn in my lifetime and I thought nothing about the monthly profits Ava reported; I trusted her.

"Is it fair to say that the demise of your firm could be due to your wife's handling of funding?"

I gritted my teeth. "Yes."

"Interesting." He picked up a sheet of paper and asked the judge if he could approach me. "Could you read this to the court please?"

"I'd rather not," I said.

“You’d rather not?” He laughed. “Mr. Hamilton, as a lawyer yourself, surely you know that you will be held in contempt for refusing to read requested evidence.”

“Read it, Mr. Hamilton.” The judge demanded.

“You’re a fucking liar, Ava.” I read my old words. “You’ve fucked so many people behind my back that I’ve lost count. As far as I’m concerned, you deserve to rot behind bars. Maybe then your overworked pussy will get a much needed break.”

A juror covered her mouth in shock, but I continued reading.

“Thank you for telling me that my cock was never up to par, that after all those years of marriage you were never satisfied… Since you and Kevin have not only managed to take away my firm, but have also ruined the one thing that made my life worth living, accept this letter as a goodbye.” I looked up at the defense.

“Could you also read what you wrote after the PS?”

I rolled my eyes. “Since you’ll only be around women for the next fifteen years, I suggest you give pussy a try. The taste is quite impeccable.”

“Objection, your honor.” The prosecutor stood up. “I don’t see how this document is relevant to the case. The defense also failed to produce that letter during discovery. I move to strike.”

“Sustained. Consider it stricken.” The judge looked at his watch and then stood up. “Let’s adjourn for lunch. Testimony will continue this afternoon.”

As the jury and the courtroom attendees filed out, I sat still. I had nowhere to go.

“I didn’t know he was going to bring up your daughter. I’m so sorry…” The prosecutor offered me a small smile. “I’ll redirect once he gets done…Your partner is definitely going down, he’s just trying to discredit your character a bit, to make him look a little more sympathetic to the jury.”

“You are aware that I’m a lawyer as well, right?” I stepped off the stand. “I know exactly what he’s trying to do.”

I stepped out of the court and outside into a heavy snowfall, looking up at the sky. I considered leaving the courthouse and risking contempt, but a part of me wanted to help seal the deal on Kevin's fate.

It'd been a long time coming—all the lies, the betrayal, the pain, and he deserved whatever he was going to get.

Someone tapped my shoulder from behind.

"You got a minute?" A familiar voice asked. Kevin.

"I don't."

"I figured…" He sighed. "Whatever happens at the end of this trial—"

"Did you not hear what I said?" I spun around to face him, taken aback by how haggard he looked up close. Time hadn't been good to him at all.

"I'm sorry for everything me and Ava put you through," he said with a genuine look in his eyes. "The money and clients were coming in so fast and we were all so young…"

"Young?"

"Yeah." He nodded. "Young and dumb, you know? It was—"

"Dumb as fuck." I clenched my jaw. "But it was more than stupidity, Kevin. It was greed. And when the newspapers started to put the pieces together, when the clients started demanding answers, you both turned on me. You blamed me…You filed for custody of Emma, knowing damn well you didn't really want her. You just wanted to hurt me since you were her biological father."

"Liam…"

"And you did." I could honestly admit that once and for all. "You really fucking did…"

"If I could take it back—"

"You can't." I cut him off. "But you can tell me one thing…"

"What is it?"

"The night you ruined my life…Well, not the first night, the night that came months later, were you drinking?"

"What does it matter now?"

"Were you fucking drinking that night?" I glared at him and he sighed, looking down at the ground.

"Yes..."

"Thank you for finally being honest." I scoffed. "I'll sleep even easier at night knowing that you'll be joining Ava behind bars after this week."

"Ava's back in prison?" He looked hurt, disappointed.

"Nine more years." I smiled, but it quickly faded. "Six more than what Emma got."

I didn't give him a chance to respond. My heart was clenching at the thought of losing Emma again, at imagining all the pain she must've felt on her last day, so I shut my eyes—trying to block another dark memory from passing by.

reasonable doubt (n.):

Not being sure of a criminal defendant's guilt to a moral certainty.

Six years ago…

Liam Henderson

Living in New York never felt ordinary. Every day there was something new to discover, something I'd never seen before.

Even though I was still running on the fumes of winning one of the biggest, yet non-reported cases in the state, I was still trying to find myself—personally and professionally. I was realizing that national popularity would always elude me, but as long as I was under-rated and not over-rated, I was perfectly fine with that.

I dropped a book of essays on my coffee table once I heard a loud knock at the door. It was a familiar loud and annoying one that my best friend Kevin always used.

"You know, you can't keep coming over in the middle of the—" I stopped talking when I realized it wasn't Kevin. It was a woman and a man, dressed in grey suits.

"Are you Liam Andrew Henderson?" The woman asked.

"Who's asking?"

"Are you Liam Andrew Henderson?" The man spoke sternly.

"Depends on who wants to know."

They both blinked.

"Yes," I said. "I'm Liam Henderson."

"You've been served." The woman thrust a thick blue envelope into my hand, the tenth time this had happened to me this week.

"Is this some type of joke? Is the *New York Times* trying to get a rise out of me again?"

They exchanged glances, confused.

"I was just doing my job," I said. "If they want to continue their pettiness by refusing to print my picture for the rest of their paper's life, that's fine. I'm okay with that, really. But serving me papers as a prank every day for a week and a half—"

"The SEC doesn't do pranks," the woman said, before they both walked away.

I shut my door and immediately called Kevin.

"This better be an emergency," he answered. "Do you know what time it is?"

"Has our firm pissed anyone off lately?"

"Of course we have. Why?"

"I just got served papers by the SEC, again."

"Have you actually opened any of the other ones?" he asked.

"Two of them," I walked over to my coffee table and pulled out a drawer. "Something about a client named Ferguson who claims we haven't been putting his money in escrow? He's suing us for five million and supposedly contacting our other clients. Do we even have a client named Ferguson?"

"We have three clients named Ferguson."

"Have we pissed any of them off?"

"Not to my knowledge." He sounded concerned. "I'm pretty sure they would've contacted us first before filing the charges, don't you think? Are you sure it's not *The New York Times* playing a mean joke on you? This is like the tenth letter you've received."

"That's the first thing I asked tonight. They said it's not them."

We were both silent for several seconds.

"It's them." We laughed in unison.

"Sorry for calling at this hour." I stuffed the envelope into the drawer with all the others. "I'll talk to you later." I hung up.

"Daddy?" Emma walked into the living room, wiping her eyes as she walked over to me. "Can I go play?"

"It's three in the morning, Emma." I shook my head. "What do you think?"

"I want to go play…" She smiled, giving me that look that made me incapable of saying no.

I smiled back and kissed her forehead, thinking of where we could possibly go out at this hour. Central Park was out of the question, as was any park, really. There was a twenty four hour donut shop nearby that we could walk to or—

I stopped mid thought. Kevin was having a special playroom built for her at the office, a room that was twice the size of his own. He'd said it would prevent me from using "I have to go check on Emma" as an excuse when we worked on demanding cases.

"I know somewhere we can go." I picked her up and carried her to her room, helping her into her favorite shoes—a pair of red rain boots she wore every day, even when it wasn't raining. "Okay, go sit on the couch so I can get dressed and then we'll go okay?"

She rushed out of her room without saying another word. I really needed to find a way to curb her wake-up-at-three-in-the-morning routine ASAP, but a part of me liked it. It was our special time together.

I put on a sweatshirt and sent my wife a quick email.

Subject: Emma.

Taking Emma out to play. Are you still at the coffee shop?

Love you,

Liam

Subject Re: Emma.
What are you going to say when she asks you for a pony?
(Yes, I'm still here...Tax season is going to be the death of me. Want me to bring you a cup back? Want to try a latte?)
I love you more,
Ava

Subject: Re: Re: Emma
Nothing. I'll just buy the pony.
(No, thank you. You know I really hate coffee.)
Impossible. I love you more than you'll ever know,
Liam

"I'm ready! I'm ready!" Emma rushed into my room, knocking over a stack of folders. "I'm ready!"

Laughing, I put my phone in my pocket and attempted to stuff the papers back in order—stopping once I saw my signature. Forged.

Confused, I sifted through the other papers-noticing the same thing.

What is this?

"Let's go, Daddy!" Emma tugged on my pants.

I tucked the folder underneath my arm and clasped her hand. "Your nap today is going to have to last for at least five hours. Do you know that?"

"I don't like naps."

"Of course you don't..." I walked her out of our apartment and to my car. As usual, Ava had slipped a note underneath the windshield wipers.

Dear Husband,
I love you—so very much, and it pains me to see you, someone with as much money and status as you have, driving a

car like this. I know you're modest, and the most expensive suit you own probably costs eighty dollars, but come on! You have to live, Liam!
I'm taking you car shopping next week and I'm not taking no for an answer,
Ava.
PS—Thank you for the roses you sent me yesterday. I got you something special and placed it on your desk at the office.

I smiled and secured Emma into her car seat, giving in when she requested to listen to her favorite song on repeat while riding to the firm.

The sleek design of the building still took people's breath away when they saw it for the first time. It was the one thing I spared no expense on when constructing; I made sure the translucent gold panels were state of the art, that the law scale statues were properly erected on marble ledges, and that the stone letters above the entrance—"Henderson & Hart" were polished every week.

And, as a giant "fuck you" to the government for burying my first case, the case that should've made me a household name and landed me on billboards all over this country, I had the office built right in front of their Social Security Office.

Pulling into the reserved parking spot, I looked in my rearview mirror—seeing that Emma was fast asleep.

Figures…

I stepped out and carried her inside anyway. I was sure she'd wake up soon.

"Good morning, Mr. Henderson." An intern greeted me as I walked inside.

"Good morning, Laura," I responded. "Am I in a different time zone today? Why is everyone awake and working right now?"

She blushed. "It's tax season."

"I keep hearing that..." I stepped onto the elevator. "I'll see you later."

Emma stirred in my arms, murmuring, but only soft snores followed.

When the elevator doors glided open, I walked through the massive "H&H" glass doors headed to Emma's half-finished playroom. I gently lowered her onto the massive pink bed and tucked her under the covers, whispering "I love you," before I dimmed the lights.

I took a seat in the corner and pulled out the folder that was under my arm, reading over what seemed like written receipts and accounts of money exchanges. Things I didn't recall doing.

I pulled out my phone to text Ava, to see if this was just another elaborate joke—something she was prone to pulling, but I heard her voice.

"Fuck!" She yelled.

I jumped up and headed to where the shouting had come from, pausing once I heard a familiar voice.

"Your pussy feels so fucking good..."

"Ahhhh...." Ava was moaning. "Just fuck me...Fuck me harder..."

I completely froze, unable to take another step. I didn't want to believe another man—Kevin, from the sound of things, was fucking my wife or that she was cheating on me.

I couldn't believe it. I trusted her way too much.

But, as she screamed a few more times—the same screams she yelled when having sex with me, I knew it was true.

"Is this how you always conduct business, *Mrs. Henderson*?" Kevin asked, laughter in his voice.

"Are you seriously going to call me that after we just fucked?" She groaned. "Can we actually get back to work now? That's the third interruption tonight and I'd actually like to get something done."

"Fine, fine..."

Papers shuffled, windows opened, but I remained frozen—still in disbelief. It wasn't until I peered through the slit of the door that my brain actually began to process what was happening.

"What are we going to do about this Ferguson shit?" Kevin asked.

"Ferguson shit? That's what we're calling it?"

"Oh, right. Here's a better name for it: Five to ten years for me. Fifteen years for you."

"I was thinking twenty."

"*Twenty*?" He slammed the table. "Are you out of your fucking mind? Twenty years? Are you suggesting that we just turn ourselves in?"

"No…" she said. "Just Liam."

"What?" He sounded appalled. "Are you joking right now?"

"Do you hear me laughing?"

Silence.

"Ava, look…" He sighed. "Liam is like a brother to me—"

"Says the man who's currently fucking his wife…Some brother you are."

"This is a mistake."

"A mistake would be one time," she said, lighting a cigarette. "Once a day for the past few years isn't necessarily the same thing. Sorry."

My heart sank.

"It was a mistake, Ava." He looked conflicted. "Tonight was going to be the last time anyway. I can't keep doing this to him."

"I don't want to stop." She walked over to the window and sighed. "I can't…"

"What?"

"He doesn't give me what I need anymore…"

"You'll have to find a way that he can. Now actually might be a good time to start, seeing as though he might have to be your lawyer."

She turned around in tears. "Is this really the last time?"

“The first time should’ve been the last time.” He walked over and massaged her shoulders. “You were only using me…You tend to forget that.”

“I wasn’t—” She choked back a sob. “I wasn’t using you…”

“Yes you were.” He kissed her lips. “And that’s okay. I sympathized.”

“Did you think I was a horrible person?

“No.”

“You promise?”

He nodded, cupping her face in his hands. “He couldn’t give you a baby and you wanted one…Naturally…That’s completely understandable.”

I held back a gasp.

“He doesn’t fuck me like you do…” she whispered.

“Stop it, Ava.” He kissed her cheek. “Stop it.”

I didn’t want to hear anymore.

I couldn’t take it.

As the two of them kissed and held each other—completely immersing themselves in their own world, I forced myself to walk away.

I hit the lights in my office and noticed a bright blue box on my desk. It read, “To: the love of my life. From: Your first and only love.”

My heart ached again as I tore the wrapping and looked inside: A new set of cufflinks, a set that probably cost more than all of my suits combined. My initials were engraved in them, and she’d enclosed a quote from my favorite authors:

“Do not be too moral. You may cheat yourself out of life much so. Aim above morality.”
-Henry David Thoreau

I sighed. She’d left out the last part of the quote, the “Be not simply good; be good for something.”

I pulled out my phone and sent her an email:

Subject: Coffee.
I think I will try some coffee...Are you still at the coffee shop?
—Liam

Subject: Re: Coffee.
Yes. I think I'll be here all night.
What kind would you like?
—Ava.

Subject: Re: Re: Coffee.
Whatever you think is best for a first timer...
Have you talked to Kevin today?
—Ava

Subject: Re: Re: Re: Coffee.
Not at all. He's been weirder than usual lately. (We really need to find him a girlfriend...) Have you?
—Ava.

I didn't answer.

I left my office and walked over to Emma's playroom, looking at her as she slept peacefully. I wanted to make her wake up, make her look at me, so I could study her features and pick them apart, so I could see for myself that she was indeed Kevin's, but I couldn't.

She was *mine*, biological father or not.

I carried her out of the firm and rushed home. As soon as I set her down, I flipped over the coffee table and opened the envelope I'd filed away hours earlier.

It was a standard summons, a demand to appear in court, but the charges listed didn't end on one page. They didn't even end on two.

It was a ten page manifesto, a laundry list of bullshit that I would never attempt: bribery, racketeering, tax fraud, mail fraud, wire fraud—every fucking fraud.

What the hell is this?

I pored over the documents for hours, my mind racing a mile a minute. Still, I couldn't completely process everything—my mind was still thinking about Kevin and Ava.

How she'd lied to me.

How he'd lied to me, too.

And now, this.

The door opened at five in the morning, and Ava set a hot cup of coffee in front of me.

"We need to talk," she said.

I said nothing. Just closed all the folders and looked at her.

"I just got served by the SEC..." She paced the floor. "Served, like *legit papers*...They came to the firm and—"

"I thought you were at the coffee shop."

"I was." She swallowed. "I stopped by the firm after getting your coffee so I could pick up a few things."

"Was anyone there with you?"

"Of course not." She scoffed. "Look at what time it is. Anyway..."

I couldn't hear anything else she was saying. I could see her lips moving, make out some of the sounds that were coming out of her mouth, but the lies she'd just told me were blocking out everything.

"Why are you cheating on me?" I blurted out, suddenly annoyed by the tears falling down her face.

She sucked in a breath and looked me up and down. "Liam, the SEC has just unreasonably served me papers. Are you seriously accusing me of infidelity right now?"

"I'm not *accusing* you. An accusation would imply that there's a chance you could be innocent. Why. Are. You. Cheating. On. Me?

She toyed with the gemstones on her necklace. Then she started to hum the refrain of a classic Sinatra song, "New York, New York."

"Don't make me ask you again, Ava," I said. "I know you've fucked Kevin."

Her eyes finally met mine. "Fine...Yes, I fucked him. Now, what?" Tears formed in her eyes. "I didn't mean for it to happen. I never thought I would cross the line with him of all people..."

"You told me Emma was a surprise..." I said. "That you didn't want to have kids until we were in our mid-thirties."

Her face paled. "You were at the office tonight weren't you?"

"I was..."

Silence.

"So," I said, mentally putting together the puzzle pieces. "Either you're lying to him about me not being able to give you a baby—because last time I checked, right before Emma was *miraculously* conceived, you were still making me wear condoms and we weren't even trying to have a fucking baby. Or, you're lying to me, and you just wanted to fuck my best friend for an ulterior motive you're saving for later. Which is it?"

"I still love you, Liam, It's just—"

"*Which is it*?"

She said nothing, she just stood there with more tears falling down her eyes.

I held up one of the folders I'd been reading through. "I was looking through these tonight...At first, I thought they were standard mail-outs that you'd signed for me while I was gone or too busy, standard office supply orders, things like that..."

"Where'd you find those?"

"But it turns out," I said, ignoring her question, "That these are all fucking favors from judges and clerks that I don't recall asking for. Ever."

"Liam..."

"Is there anyone in this city that you haven't fucked to get something in return?"

She looked as if she actually had to think about it.

"I send you flowers every day—every. fucking. day." I stepped forward. "I tell you that I love you and that you complete me, every day and this is what I get in return?"

"I understand how you feel, Liam, but—"

"No, you don't fucking understand." I clenched my fists. "I've never even entertained the thought of being *friends* with another woman. I make sure everyone knows I'm completely unavailable, that no one else stands a damn chance."

"I cheated for your benefit, Liam. I did it for you."

What the fuck?

I'd heard a lot of bullshit in my life, but that line officially took the cake.

"How do you think you won the Luttrell case?" She wiped away her tears and narrowed her eyes at me. "You think you did it with your award winning rhetoric and charm?"

"Do you have a mental disorder that you failed to tell me about?"

"I fucked the judge three days before the verdict. You were going to lose. And if you lost that case, there's no way some of our current clients would've picked our firm to handle their account."

"*Our* firm?"

"You think you built it alone?" She laughed. "Liam Henderson, warm-hearted, loyal, and too nice for his own fucking good? Please. I had to intercept every contract you sent out and redraft half of the terms. If I'd left it up to you, your firm would be nothing more than a pipe dream. You should be thanking me because you have no idea how much work I've done to put you where you are."

"You've never argued a single case."

"No, but I've fucked a lot of powerful people to make sure you never lost one."

"I've never lost because I'm a damn good lawyer."

"And I'm a damn good lay." She shrugged. "Of course, my own husband has been so busy this year that he probably wouldn't even know."

"You're blaming me for throwing your pussy around?"

"I'm shocked you even know what the word *pussy* means." She hissed. "We lay in bed together every night and you never want to fuck me."

"You always say that you're tired. Or is that a lie, too?"

"I was only tired of fucking you." She brushed past me and shut the door to Emma's room. "What do you want to do now, huh? Divorce me?"

"Is that a serious question?"

"It is." She smirked and a knock came to the door.

We both stood rooted to the floor, and the knock came again.

"I'll get it." I warned. "You stay there."

I walked away and opened it, expecting to see Kevin so I could punch the shit out of him, but it was a different woman in a suit.

A young blonde.

"You've um…" Her cheeks reddened. "You've been…"

"*Served*!" Someone whispered loudly from around the corner. "Tell him he's been *served*…"

"You're an intern at *The New York Times*, aren't you?" I rolled my eyes.

She nodded, but then she added. "My boss says you can go fuck yourself, and that even though we'll never run your picture, we'll make sure everyone knows that your firm is about to be run into the ground starting tomorrow." She handed me the copy print for an article in tomorrow's paper. "He says it's your turn to feel some karma."

I slammed the door in her face.

"I think you need to seriously weigh your options before you act out on your emotions." Ava was right behind me, holding a sleeping Emma.

"Is this a threat?"

"It's a promise…"

I raised my eyebrow. "And what exactly are the proposed terms?"

"If you help me sort this thing out—if you get the SEC off the firm's back, both of us can avoid serving any time."

"I'm not serving any fucking time. I didn't do anything wrong. And if you think I won't be the first person in line to help the state put your ass away, you're sadly fucking mistaken."

"Awww." She pouted. "Look at you. Trying to sound all masculine and tough for a change, sounding like the man I wish you could've been."

"Fuck you, Ava."

"Not a chance." She narrowed her eyes at me. "Let me try phrasing this another way: I know that you're Mr. Lawyer of the Year and you'd never willingly lie because you have a conscience and all that. But if you don't help me, or if you refuse to tell investigators that you were partly responsible for what happened—that we *all* played a small part, I'm filing for sole custody of Emma."

"File away. No judge in his right mind would give you sole custody."

She laughed. "This is actually why people fuck to get what they want, *honey*. It comes in handy for times like this. Besides, you're not even her real father." She kissed Emma's forehead. "Did you overhear that part while you were watching us fuck or were you too busy taking notes?"

I didn't get a chance to answer.

"Do not fuck with me, Liam." She hissed. "You have no idea how far I'm willing to go to stay out of prison."

"Even though you deserve to be there?" I snatched Emma away from her, making her stir. "You sought out clients using my name and you misappropriated the money. For what?"

"Status. Something you'll never understand."

"Something you'll never need." I countered. "Everyone behind bars shares the same level of popularity."

She rolled her eyes. "I'm going to give you a few days to come to your senses."

"Or else what?"

"You don't want to know the answer to that." She walked out, slamming the door behind her—waking Emma.

She looked at me with her bright blue eyes, smiling. "Can I go play?"

I nodded, unable to even speak. Carrying her to the balcony, I didn't even bother grabbing an umbrella for myself. I set her down and helped her into a coat, trying not to think about what Ava could possibly have up her sleeve.

Emma tilted her head up to the sky and swallowed raindrops, and then she dashed away from me—running in circles.

A loud thunder roared in the distance, and as if she could tell what I was about to say, she looked at me with a wide grin. "Five more minutes!"

—

The New York Times didn't waste any time printing the story. Well, stories.

Henderson & Hart, Revered Law Firm, Embroiled in Scandal.
Hart Agrees to Cooperate Against Henderson, Following Brutal Bar Brawl.
Henderson Arrested, Questioned, After Wife Claims Recent Domestic Abuse.

The only story they didn't mention, out of a hanging thread of respect, was my losing custody of Emma. Of me having to hand her over to Kevin.

I was innocent of every charge I faced, but due to the fact that I'd bashed Kevin's head in, and Ava had claimed I was just as violent with her, it left the judge no choice but to put her in custody with her supposed "loving and biological father per the mother's request."

I thought it would only be for a week or two, a month at most, but as the charges piled up and the cases were trudged through the courts at a snail's pace, the months wore on and on.

To make matters worse, Kevin and Ava purposely took Emma to places they knew I frequented: My favorite place at Central Park, my spot on the Brooklyn Bridge, my favorite restaurants.

In between my court appearances, I followed them to the park—resisting the urge to yell at them for letting her get too close to the streets, holding back the urge to take her back and flee the state.

Instead, I filed injunction after injunction—fighting multiple cases at once. I searched through every loophole of custody, documenting cases after case of non-biological fathers retaining rights.

Eventually the truth about Ava and Kevin's scheme began to surface, and on the same day that Ava confessed to lying about me beating her—when she admitted that she'd made that all up, I won custody of Emma.

It was three days before her fourth birthday, so I arranged for a few of her neighborhood friends to come by with their parents. The theme was the rainforest, of course, and the party favors were umbrellas and rain-boots.

Kevin, still foolishly proclaiming his innocence in regards to the fraud, had grown quite attached to her over the past few months. He asked if he could still see her on the weekends once he returned her to me, but I didn't even bother answering that question.

He'd seen her long enough.

Standing outside my brownstone, I called him two hours before her birthday party, making sure he was still dropping her off on time. Instead of talking to me like an adult, he made Emma repeat his every word to me.

"We'll be there soon," she said, a smile in her soft voice. "Can you please let us enjoy our last few hours alone? She's my daughter, too."

"See you soon, Emma."

"Goodbye, Daddy!" She hung up and I rearranged the party decorations for the umpteenth time, greeting the early guests and directing them into the living room.

Half an hour passed.

A whole hour.

Two.

I called Kevin, annoyed that he was pulling this bullshit of a stunt—as if it was even *half* as difficult as it had been for me, but there was no answer.

Upset, I dialed the police and they showed up to my door within minutes.

"Are you Liam Henderson?" They asked.

"Yes, I'm the one that called."

I pulled the court order out of my pocket and explained what was happening, how Kevin was technically committing kidnapping, but they interrupted me.

They weren't at my house to take a report.

They were there to give one.

As they calmly explained what had happened, how she was less than a block away when the car collided with a truck, my world stopped.

I asked which hospital she was being flown to, which route was the fastest to take, but the cops simply sighed and looked past me, as if they didn't want to say anything further.

They didn't have to.

Their looks said it all.

Emma's funeral was held on a grey and wet day, another harsh blow to my chest. I sat through speeches from the few people she'd crossed paths with, from her young friends who had yet to fully comprehend what her death really meant.

My next door neighbor, a four year old named Hannah, said, "I hope you come back next week, Emma. You can come to my birthday party."

I stared at the tiny casket as they lowered it into the ground, half of me wanting to jump in with it and risk being buried alive. At least then I wouldn't have to feel anything anymore.

As the crowd dissipated one by one—tapping my shoulder and saying, "I'm so sorry for your loss," as they left, I spotted Ava walking into the cemetery.

Flanked by two prison guards, she fell to her knees and bawled once she reached the uncovered grave.

"You made me late for my child's funeral." She cursed at the guards. "I fucking missed it…How cruel can you possibly be?"

"All furloughs have the same time constraints, ma'am," one of them said flatly. "We couldn't have left any earlier."

She shook her head and continued to cry, beating her hands against the ground. As if she needed to distance herself from the guilt, she stood up and walked towards the podium, reading the papers that were left behind.

She broke down again and I walked over.

"Liam…" She held out her arms. "She's really gone, isn't she?"

"*She is.*" I refused to console her. "And it's all your fault, Ava. Your fucking fault."

"Don't you think I know that?" She sniffled. "Don't you think I *feel* that?"

"It should be you down there in the ground right now. It should be you."

"Liam..."

"She didn't deserve to be taken away from me and you know it."

"I do know that...I was just—"

"Trying to prove a point? To do whatever it took to hurt me because you fucked yourself over and you wanted to bring me down with you?"

"We can get through this...We can still find a way to restore your name in this city, and you're the best lawyer I know so...I know you can turn everything around and maybe help me too. Maybe forgive me?"

"I'm going to do everything in my power to make sure you rot in prison, to make sure you never get out and that the parole board never gives you an ounce of sympathy."

"You don't mean that, Liam..."

"If I ever find a way to get away with murder, you and Kevin will be my first victims."

The guard across from us gave me a look.

"Don't be like this, Liam..."

"My name won't be Liam for too much longer just so you know. It'll be Andrew."

"Are you leaving? Are you about to leave me here?"

"That should be you in the ground right now..." I noticed the funeral director stacking the chairs, mindlessly breaking down what was just another ceremony to him. "That should be you..."

One of the guards began speaking with the funeral staff, inquiring as to whether they should leave the premises or not. Noticing her time here was limited, Ava grabbed onto me. "Liam, I mean...*Andrew*. You clearly still love me because you're trusting me with that...We can rebuild everything we had, we can start over, you and me...We can do this if you help me..."

I grabbed her hands and moved them away as one of the guards stepped closer.

"You know I don't belong in prison," she said, crying. "They're transferring me to a permanent location next week...Save me, Andrew...Save me..."

I said nothing.

"If I could take everything back, I swear...I swear I would. Don't you think I love Emma, too?"

"Loved," I said. "It's past tense now, don't you think?"

She sighed. "Please don't leave me..."

"I won't." I stepped back so the guards could escort her back to the van. "I'll write..."

"Really?" Her eyes looked hopeful as she walked away. "Okay, I look forward to your letters...I look forward to fixing us..."

The rain picked up its pace, transitioning from a drizzle to a downpour, but I remained standing—unable to walk away from Emma. I re-read her tiny tombstone, crying as her face crossed my mind.

Emma Rose Henderson,
A Daddy's girl, through and through.
Gone too soon,
But never forgotten...

I stared at those words for hours, letting the rain drench me to the bone. It wasn't until the director informed me that the gates were closing, that I walked away.

Lost and heartbroken, I spent the next few months in a dizzying haze. Despite the fact that Ava was the one behind bars, the paper continued spouting her lies as facts, slandering me, and I didn't even bother disputing it.

I didn't have the energy.

I submitted written testimonies through lawyers I'd hired—knowing that eventually things would sort themselves out. I didn't even care that Ava had hired her own high profile team to block me from getting a divorce.

I no longer gave a fuck about anything.

My firm collapsed before my very eyes—everything down to the sink-ware was sold off in parts, and in the legal community, the downfall became a warning, a tell-tale of what happened when status and greed consumed one of us.

I drank every morning, letting the alcohol numb my pain. And whenever I awoke from passing out, I drank again. It was only when I started drinking coffee that I could somewhat function well enough to get anything done.

Visiting the cemetery was too painful, almost as painful as stepping inside Emma's room. So, I hired a few people to pack it away in boxes, telling them to leave out the "E" and "H" frames; I could bear to look at those since she'd hand-picked them.

For months, I mourned the life she would never have—attempting to make sense of it all. I knew deep down that I couldn't stay here, but I couldn't leave as the same man that I was; I knew that I'd never get over Emma, but I needed a way to cope. A way to slowly re-integrate myself into the real world.

Stopping by a newspaper stand, my eyes caught an article about the newest hotshot lawyer in town—Michael Weston. Dressed in one of the expensive suits that Kevin once raved about, he was the talk of the city and from the words I was reading, he was cocky—only slightly cockier than I had become recently.

"Oh, you got the last one…" A woman said as she stepped next to me.

"You want this paper?"

"Well…" She blushed. "Not really the paper. I just want the ad of Michael Weston so I can show my friends my ideal dream guy."

"Have you read some of the shit he's said in this interview?" I raised my eyebrow. "He's an asshole."

"That just makes him more loveable, don't you think."

"They asked him what he does when he gets less than favorable reviews." I couldn't believe how fucking gullible this woman looked. "Do you want to know what he said?"

"Sure." She crossed her arms. "What does he do when he gets bad reviews?"

"He looks at his bank account," I said. "And then he claims, and I quote, 'I don't recall learning that someone needs to be well-liked in order to be successful.' He really said that."

She practically melted into the sidewalk. "I bet he really knows how to fuck..."

I gave her the paper and walked away. Her bringing up sex was a reminder of how long it'd been since I slept with someone.

And then it hit me: Sex.

I needed some, badly.

I signed up for an online dating site, Date-Match, and slowly shed the layers of the man I used to be. I bought expensive suits—one for every day of the week. I slowly curbed my excessive drinking to make room for a new appetite, and instead of punching my walls to de-stress, I invested in Cuban cigars.

Still, the women I met online were average, and none of them seemed to be about sex. They just wanted to talk about bullshit—always leaving me restless and alone at the end of the night to drink away my sorrows; forcing me back to square one with my experiment.

Like the woman who was sitting on the edge of the bed right now, a goddamn mile-a-minute talker. She was a few years older than me, a teacher of some sort, and she couldn't shut up for shit.

She was talking about her life in college, about some boy named Billy she once loved—some boy who never loved her back. Before she could start elaborating about the campus bond-fire where the two of them met, I realized that I couldn't take this shit anymore.

"Billy and I would've been perfect together, I think," she said. "There was even this one time that—"

"Are we going to fuck or what?" I cut her off.

"*What*?" She clutched her chest. "What did you just say?"

"I said, are we going to fuck *or what*?" I emphasized every syllable. "I didn't reserve this hotel room so I could sit and listen to you talk all night."

Her jaw dropped.

"I thought that..." She stuttered. "I thought that you liked me."

"I like you enough to fuck you. That's about it."

Her eyes went wide and she stepped back. "All this time that we've been dating you've only been thinking about sleeping with me?"

I mentally added "rhetorical questions" to the list of shit I wasn't going to put up with anymore.

"I was under the impression that all those dates you took me on was because—"

"I took you on all those dates so we could scratch the surface of each other's personalities. So I could know that you're not some psycho-murderer, and so you could be assured that I'm not one either." I grimaced at all the time I'd clearly wasted. "The purpose was so the both of us could be comfortable enough to fuck, and then after that we could go our separate ways."

"It was only going to be *once*?"

"Do you have a hearing problem?"

She looked completely lost, and I wasn't in the mood to make this picture any clearer.

Before I could say another word, she looked into my eyes.

"So," she said, still in shock, "all the things on your profile were a lie?"

"No. Everything on my profile is one hundred percent accurate." I pulled out my phone. "I specifically wrote what I'm in for, and I've been more than lenient spending my time with you. You seem like a nice person, but after tonight—whether we fuck or not, I won't be speaking to you again. So, what's it going to be?"

She stood there, her jaw dropped once more, and I glanced at my profile.

Sure enough, I'd forgotten to adjust the default settings when I'd signed up for Date-Match, and my "What I'm Looking For" box was still set to bullshit: "Long conversations, a connection with someone I can truly relate to, and finding my one true love."

Ha...

I quickly erased all of the text and looked up, noticing that my date for tonight was still in the room.

"If you continue standing here," I said," I'm going to assume that you do want to fuck tonight. If not, the door's right behind you."

The sound of her huffing was the last sound I heard before the door slammed so hard it rattled the mirror on the wall.

Unfazed, I contemplated what I wanted to write in my profile's box. Over the past few months, I'd found disappointment after disappointment—wasting too much of my time and money on women who were not on the same wavelength as me.

And now it all made perfect sense. All those unnecessary dinners, late night conversations, and utter bullshit was about to end right now.

I didn't need another relationship—those days were gone forever, and I would never spend more than a week talking to the same woman on the phone.

As the sun set outside the hotel room's window, the perfect phrasing came to me, and I typed: One dinner. One night. No repeats.

Then I highlighted it and placed it in bold.

Staring at it, I realized how bare it looked, how someone might actually think I wasn't dead ass serious, so underneath, I made things completely clear:

Casual sex. Nothing more. Nothing less.

condone (v.):

To forgive, support, and/or overlook moral or legal failures of another without protest, with the result that it appears that such breaches of moral or legal duties are acceptable. An employer may overlook an employee overcharging customers or a police officer may look the other way when a party uses violent self-help to solve a problem

Aubrey

I sat in the back of the courtroom, listening to Andrew break down on the stand. Twice, when the defense purposely brought up Emma, he lost all composure.

Yet, as I saw the look in his eyes at the mere mention of her, of the "slip" of her name, I felt his pain.

I kept my head down the remainder of his testimony so our eyes wouldn't meet, so he wouldn't know I was here, and when the judge called for a short recess, I slipped outside.

Reporters were murmuring in the hallway, hoping he didn't read any of their old articles about him years ago, and suddenly they were shouting questions.

"Mr. Henderson! Mr. Henderson!" They hounded him the second he stepped outside of the courtroom. "Mr. Henderson!"

He stopped and looked at them. "My name is *Mr. Hamilton*."

"How do you feel about potentially sending your former partner and best friend away to prison?"

"He's sending himself to prison," he answered.

"Do you have any intentions of reconnecting with him while he's behind bars?"

He ignored that question with a blank stare.

"Your name was cleared years ago and yet you still left New York," someone else asked. "Now that everything is in the open for good, any chance that you'll come back and re-open your firm?"

"I'm about to spend my last hour in this city on the way to the airport," he said, pulling shades over his eyes.

The throng of reporters followed him out of the courtroom, and he slipped inside the car without a second glance.

Sighing, I pulled out my phone and re-read the messages he'd sent me this morning, somewhat regretting that I didn't respond.

Subject: NYC.
I would like to see you one last time before I leave. Can I pick you up for breakfast?
PS—I really was going to tell you everything that night…
—Andrew

Subject: Your Pussy.
This message is actually not about your pussy. (Although, since I'm on the subject, it is number one on my list of favorite things.)
Come to breakfast with me. I'm outside your door.
—Andrew

As I was rereading that email, a new one popped onto my screen:

Subject: Goodbye.
—Andrew

I knew my lack of response was immature, that it was my fault that I didn't get to see him before he left, but I felt as if he could've made more of an effort. And I still felt that he was wrong for not being open with me when he should have.

Leaving the courthouse, I headed home and thought about all the half-truths and lies that had swirled our relationship. Alyssa. His wife. My real name. His real name.

Everything we had was built on lies…

Letting tears roll down my face, I opened the door to my house, prepared to shower until I couldn't cry anymore, but Andrew was standing in my living room.

"Hello, Aubrey." He glared at me.

"Breaking and entering is a crime." I crossed my arms. "Shouldn't you know that?"

He said nothing, just continued glaring at me—looking me up and down.

"Don't you have a flight to catch?" My voice cracked. "Shouldn't you be spending your last hour in New York on the way to the airport?"

"I realized I still have something to say to you."

"Do you have another fake name you want to tell me about? Another secret identity that you want to—"

"Stop." He stepped closer and closer until I backed into a wall, and he looked directly into my eyes. "I need you to listen to me, Aubrey. Just fucking listen…"

I tried to move away from him, but he grabbed my hands and pinned them above my head. Then he used his hips to keep me still.

"You're going to stand here and listen to me for the next five minutes whether you like it or not." The words came out rushed, heated. "Since you suddenly care about knowing the truth, I'll tell you the fucking truth..."

I tried to say something, but he leaned down and bit my lips. Hard.

"I liked you when you were Alyssa and I was Thoreau—when we spent nights talking about your ridiculous homework and my law firm...I even liked you after you fucking lied to me and I saw you at your interview—I *liked* you..." He tightened his grip around my wrists. "And even though I knew I shouldn't have chased you down and showed up to your apartment that day, I did, and I fucked you...After that, I *really* liked you."

"Are you being serious right now?"

"Dead ass serious." He glared at me and bit my lips again, silently commanding me to keep quiet. "I didn't want to like you, Aubrey. I wasn't supposed to, and I didn't need to, but every day after that you were all I could think about. You and your smartass mouth, and how your lies maybe weren't so bad after all."

"What about *your lies*? Do you still think that you're above morality? That—"

"*Stop talking.*" He choked out. "Let me finish."

I swallowed and he stared at me a few seconds before continuing.

"Yes, I hid the fact that I was married from you, and although it was unintentional, it was still a lie."

"A *huge* lie."

"*Aubrey...*" He gripped me tighter. "I hadn't thought about Ava in a very long time...On the contrary, I've been thinking about you every day since you left."

"No, you haven't..."

"I have." He looked directly into my eyes. "I drove to your ballet class twice a week, trying to see you, trying to talk to you and apologize...I sent things to your apartment. I even showed up twice, but that was before I knew you'd moved."

"You're just saying all this so you can fuck me..." I shook my head and turned away, but he made me face him again.

"I'm saying all of this because I love you..."

I gasped and tears formed in my eyes.

"I fucking love you, Aubrey..." he repeated, wiping my face. "And I'll do whatever it takes to show you that." He brushed his lips against mine. "Do you still love me?"

"No, I don't...Not any—" I felt his lips against mine, silencing me.

I didn't want to kiss him back, I wanted to push him away and tell him to leave, but I parted my lips and let his tongue slip inside of my mouth.

Slowly, he freed my hands from his grip and locked his arms around my waist—keeping his lips attached to mine. He didn't give me a chance to talk, to breathe. He just kissed me senseless until I couldn't take it anymore.

"If you can honestly say that you don't love me," he whispered, slowly pulling away from me, "then I'll leave you alone."

"And if I can't?" I asked, breathless.

"If you can't, you're going to show me to your room so you and I can become reacquainted."

"Reacquainted?" I moaned as he cupped my ass. "Is that code for conversation?"

"It's code for fucking."

"Would it kill you to say make love just once?"

"Depends on if you actually love me or not."

Silence.

His fingers were now trailing the zipper on the back of my skirt, gently pulling on it as I looked into his eyes.

"I hate you," I said, making him raise his eyebrow. "If you said all of those things just to get my hopes up, I'll never forgive you."

"You still haven't..." He kissed me gently. "I meant every word I said." He pulled my zipper down. "And I really need to know whether or not you still love me because..." He stopped talking.

My skirt fell into a puddle on the floor and he tugged my thong away from my waist until it snapped.

"Aubrey, tell me…Tell me right now."

I gasped as he slipped a finger inside of me, as he groaned at how wet I was.

"Yes…"

"Yes?" He moved his finger in and out. "Yes, what?"

"Yes, I—" I paused as he kissed my lips. "Yes, I still love you."

"Where's your bedroom?"

I looked to my left and he immediately tugged me down the hall, shutting the door behind us. He didn't give me a chance to get undressed. His hands were all over me—unbuttoning my shirt, ripping my bra, and caressing my breasts.

I reached forward and unbuckled his pants, pushing his pants down. Then he tossed me onto the bed, climbing on top of me.

I spread my legs beneath him, lifting my hips up so he could fuck me, but he didn't. Instead he kissed my neck—whispering how much he missed me, how much he needed me.

"Andrew…" I felt his cock rubbing against my thigh.

He slowly moved his mouth to my chest—swirling his tongue across my nipples as he palmed my breasts. His kisses traveled further and further, all the way down to my thighs.

I shut my eyes as he pressed his tongue against my clit, as he teasingly darted it against me in slow, sensuous circles.

"Ahhhh…" I tried to clamp my legs shut, but he pinned them to the mattress and looked up at me.

"Aubrey…" His voice was low.

"Yes?"

He circled his thumb around my clit, making it swell in pleasure. "Tell me that I own this."

I shut my eyes as he increased the pressure, rubbing his thumb around and around.

"Tell me that I own your pussy, Aubrey."

"Yes..." I writhed underneath his hand. "Yes..."

"Say it." He prevented me from rolling over. "I need you to say it."

Tingles traveled up and down my spine and I finally stared back at him. "Yes...You own it."

He smiled and pressed his head between my legs again, devouring me—making me scream at the top of my lungs, but he didn't let me cum.

Instead, he flipped me over. "Get down on all fours."

I caught my breath and slowly obliged, and the next thing I felt was him palming my ass, kissing his way down my spine.

"I still haven't claimed every inch of you..." he said, squeezing my cheeks harshly. "But I'll save that for when I think you're ready..."

I murmured as he slid into my pussy inch by inch, making me lean forward. He took the elastic out of my hair and pulled me back, whispering, "It's going to feel just like this...Maybe even better..."

"Ahhhh..."

"And when it happens, you're going to let me cum inside of you..." His other hand skimmed my sides and squeezed my breasts. "I want you to feel every last drop..."

"Andrew." I gripped the sheets.

"Yes?"

I didn't answer. I couldn't.

He was slapping my ass as he pounded into me, giving it to me rough as he whispered my name.

I met him thrust for thrust, unable to let go of the sheets, and when I felt myself nearing the edge—coming close to it as he tortured my clit with his fingers, he denied me once again.

He pulled out of me, making me whimper, and then he made me face him once again. Immediately burying himself inside of me, he stared into my eyes—slowly sliding his cock back and forth, suffocating my screams with his mouth.

I felt his cock throbbing inside of me, felt my muscles clenching as he cursed against my lips and as we locked eyes again, we both came at the same time.

I fell forward against his chest, panting. "Andrew, I…"

He cut me off with a kiss. "I love you, too…"

We lay there connected for what felt like forever—him threading his fingers through my hair, me rubbing my hands against his chest.

"Are you okay?" he asked.

"Yes…"

He rolled out of bed and stood up to toss away the condom. "Come here."

I couldn't move. I was still feeling weak from my last orgasm.

He shook his head and slipped his hands underneath my thighs, picking me up and carrying me out of the room, checking each door we passed. When we reached the bathroom, he set me down on the floor.

"I don't think I can stand up long enough for a shower…" I whispered.

He ignored me and turned on the water. "We're not going to take a shower." He picked me up and gently placed me into the tub.

Climbing in behind me, he grabbed an empty bottle and filled it with warm water. Then he gently poured it over my head.

He grabbed some shampoo from the ledge and squirted a few drops into my hair, lathering it to suds.

I heard him asking me questions, something about how I was feeling or if I wanted to talk to him about whatever I had on my mind, but as his fingers continued to massage my scalp, everything went black.

———

I woke up in bed alone.

There was no note from Andrew, and all of his clothes were gone.

I was starting to think having sex with him was all a dream, but I spotted his wallet sitting on top of my nightstand. I pulled the covers off of me and smiled once I saw that he'd dressed me in a silk slip.

I made my way out of the room and down the hallway where he was standing out on my balcony smoking a cigar.

"Since when do you smoke?" I stepped behind him.

"I don't often," he said. "Only when I need to think."

I nodded and looked out into the night sky, but I suddenly felt him pulling me against him.

"Aren't you going to ask what I'm thinking about?" He smirked. "Surely you have questions."

"I do, *Liam*."

"We can talk about it."

"Now?"

"If that's what you want…" He put out his cigar and walked me over to a chair, pulling me into his lap. "How long have you known about that?"

"A couple weeks…"

"Hmmm."

I shook my head. "Do Bach and Greenwood know who you really are?"

"They do."

"So, why do you have to hide it from everyone else?"

"Esteemed lawyer or not, no one wants to take on someone who has a history in the papers…It makes a high profile firm look bad." He kissed the back of my shoulder.

"What was Emma like?"

He sighed, looking at me. "She was perfect…"

I thought of a way to change the subject, but he continued talking.

"She hated when I went to work, and she would beg me to come sometimes, so I'd let her…" His voice was low. "And then I wouldn't get any work done because the park was right across the street and she always wanted to play…Always."

"Did she follow you around at home?" I asked.

"She was my shadow. She would come sleep on the couch if I was up working, and if she saw me leave the room to take a call, she would cross her arms and look offended if I didn't invite her to listen." He let out a short laugh, but he didn't say anything else.

"Can I ask you something?" I leaned against his chest.

"If I say no I don't think it'll stop you…"

"Where do we go from here?"

"What do you mean?"

"I mean…What happens now with us?"

He looked at me, confused. "*Us*?"

"Are we in a relationship? Are you going to stay with me, or are you going back to Date-Match?"

He stared at me for a long time. "I can't stay in New York, Aubrey. I think you can understand why…"

"You had no plans to stay past tonight did you?"

"No."

"And you leave in the morning?"

"Yes." He tried to kiss my hair, but I moved away. "So, was this some type of way to get your Aubrey fix before you went home? Say all the right things so you can feel better about yourself when you leave?"

"I wanted you to know that I loved you before I went home."

"And to get some pussy on the side, of course."

"Of course." He smirked, but I didn't return his smile.

"I told you not to get my hopes up, Andrew." I stepped back. "And you did it anyway."

"What do you want me to do, Aubrey? Move in with you? Fucking propose?"

"I want you to stay…And if you can't stay, I want you to leave…Now."

"Aubrey..."

"*Now*," I said. "We can still be friends, but I don't want to—"

"Stop." He pulled me close and pressed his mouth against mine. "We're more than friends...We always were. I just can't be with you right now."

I opened my mouth to protest, but he kissed me again and again, whispering as he cupped my breasts, "I would really prefer if we spent the rest of night in bed and not arguing..."

adjourn (v.):

To suspend proceedings: to suspend the business of a court, legislature, or committee indefinitely.

Weeks later…

Aubrey

I stood on my toes backstage—tilting my head toward the ceiling, rehearsing the final move of the production one last time. I should've been happy and smiling—overjoyed at the fact that I was about to debut in the leading role in a New York Ballet Company production, but I wasn't. Far from it.

I felt alone, and I knew no amount of applause or accolades would take those feelings away.

I was still hanging onto my last few moments with Andrew: The early morning sex in the shower, the sex against my door, the sex in the town car on the way to the airport. (And there was also the final romp in the airport's bathroom…)

He told me that he loved me each time—that he didn't want to leave me, but he left anyway.

Our relationship was now relegated to talking on the phone every night—recapping our days, getting off on each other's fantasies in between, but it wasn't enough. And I knew it wasn't going to be enough for me for too much longer.

I needed him here.

"Forty minutes everyone!" A stage hand slipped past me. "Places in forty!"

I took a deep breath and walked to a mirror that hung near the wing. Staring at myself, I looked over tonight's costume—a glimmering white visage that looked like it'd been plucked from a dream: Sparkling crystals adorned every inch of the leotard, the tutu was freshly fluffed and sprayed with glitter, and my feathered headband was far more defined and layered than the one I'd worn in Durham.

"Aubrey?" A familiar voice said from behind.

"Mom?" I spun around. "What are you doing backstage?"

"We wanted to come and tell you good luck in person." She nodded at my father.

"Thank you…"

"We also want you to know that despite the fact that we still wish you'd pursued law school, we're very proud of you for pursuing your own dreams."

I smiled. "Thank you, again."

"And we are also very, *very* honored to have you as our daughter because you're such an inspiration to all the college students who will be heading to the polls in this year's election—students who have similar dreams and ambitions regarding careers in the arts."

"*What*?"

"Did you get all that?" She turned to the reporter behind us who was shutting off his device. "Make sure you use that last part as a sound bite for the next commercial."

"*Seriously*?"

"What?" She shrugged. "I meant every word of that, but it's also good to get it on tape, don't you think?"

I didn't bother with a rebuttal.

My father stepped over and hugged me, posing for an unnatural photo-op, but when the photographer walked away he smiled.

"I'm happy for you, Aubrey," he said. "I think this is where you belong."

"You're just saying that because you think me being here means I won't mess up the campaign at home."

"No, I *know* you being here means you won't mess up the campaign at home." He laughed. "But I'm still happy for you."

"How reassuring…"

"It's true," my mother chimed in. "We're excited for you."

"Ladies and gentlemen we are about to begin our show in exactly one hour!" Mr. Ashcroft bellowed. "If you are not a ballerina, a danseur, or a stagehand please find your way off my stage. Now!"

My parents embraced me—holding onto me for a long time. As they pulled back, they took turns kissing my cheek before they walked away.

I adjusted my headband one last time and checked my phone. Sure enough, there was an email. Andrew.

Subject: Good luck.
I'm sorry I couldn't make it to your first opening night, but I look forward to hearing about it tonight when you call me.
I'm sure you'll be quite memorable to everyone in the audience.
—Andrew.
PS—I miss you.

Subject: Re: Good luck.
I am not calling you tonight. You should've been here. I'll *think* about recapping it for you next week.
—Aubrey.
PS—You "missing me" would be a lot more convincing if the subject of the email you sent two hours ago wasn't "I miss your pussy."

Subject: Re: Re: Good luck.
I know I should've been there. Hence the aforementioned apology.
And you *will* call me.
—Andrew
PS—I miss you both.

Subject: Re: Re: Re: Good luck.
I really wanted you to be here…
—Aubrey

I turned off my phone so I wouldn't have to continue messaging him. I needed to focus.

All the rehearsals and dance lessons I'd taken over the past twenty two years had brought me to this moment. In thirty six minutes, my every move would be on display for one of the biggest audiences in the dance world.

It would draw critiques from the staunchest critics—the most advent admirers of ballet, and the papers would run early reviews that could make or break the remaining production run. But right now, in this moment, none of that mattered.

This was my dream, I was finally living it, and I could only make sure I was the best I could possibly be.

"Are you ready, Miss Everhart?" Mr. Ashcroft placed his hands on my shoulders. "Are you ready to show this city that you belong here?"

I nodded. "Very much so, sir."

"Good, because I'm ready for them to see that, too." He clapped his hands above his head, signaling the rest of the dancers to circle us.

"Ladies and gentlemen, it is officially opening night," he said. "You've worked hard for months, logged every necessary hour and then some, and I do believe that tonight's execution of *Swan*

Lake will be the best execution this audience will ever see." He paused. "If it isn't, I'll make sure you pay for it at tomorrow morning's rehearsal."

There were groans. We knew he wasn't kidding.

"I'll be sitting in the balcony at center stage, and I will not give you one clap, no inkling of applause, if the show is anything less than perfect. Are we clear?"

"Yes sir." We collectively murmured, still intimidated by his power.

"Good. Take your places now." He walked away from us and snapped his fingers. "Make me proud."

I took my place at center stage and turned my back to the curtain—raising my hands above my head. I heard the orchestra giving their instruments one final tuning, heard the pianist replaying the refrain he missed at this morning's rehearsal, and then I heard silence.

Ear deafening silence.

The lights in the gallery flickered, slow at first then faster, and everything went black.

Five....Four...Three...Two...

The pianist played the first stanza of the composition and the curtains rose, cueing the spotlight to shine against my back.

The swan corps—twenty ballerinas dressed in complementing white tutus, formed a circle around me, and as they stood on their toes, tilting their heads back, I slowly turned around to face the audience—pausing, taking all of the nameless faces in, and then I became lost in my own world.

I was Odette, The Swan Queen, and I was falling in love with a prince at first sight, dancing with him underneath a glittering orb of lights, telling him he needed to pledge his love for me if he wanted to break my lake's spell.

The gasps from the audience could be heard over the music, but I kept my focus.

I seamlessly transitioned from the white, sweet swan who wanted nothing more than to fall in love, into the black, evil swan—Odile, who wanted nothing more than to prevent it from happening.

I illustrated love, heartbreak, and devastation over the course of two hours, never stopping to catch my breath, never missing a beat.

In the final frame, where the love of my life vows to die with me instead of honoring his mistaken promise to the black swan, I can't help but deviate from the choreography.

Instead of taking his hand and letting him lead me into the "water," I leapt into his arms—letting him hold me high for all the other swans to see. And then the two of us spun into oblivion—"dying" together.

The music began its decrescendo—half-somber, half-light, and the lights shut off—leaving nothing. Ending everything with blackness.

And silence.

All of a sudden, a raucous applause arose from the audience and a collection of cheers—"Bravo!" "Encore!" "Bravissimo!" echoed off the walls.

The stage lights brightened and I took a bow, looking out into a sea of well-entertained faces: Mr. Petrova was front and center, nodding as he clapped, mouthing, "Good job, good job." My mother was wiping a tear from her eye and looking up at my father, saying, "That's our daughter." Even Mr. Ashcroft, still stone faced, was standing and applauding, stopping once his eyes met mine.

"Bravo." He mouthed before turning away.

I kept a smile plastered on my face as I scanned the room, looking for the one person I wanted—the one person I *needed* to see, but he wasn't there.

"Thank you ladies and gentlemen for attending our opening night," one of the directors said as she took the stage. "Per our opening night tradition, we will now introduce the members of our corps to you..."

I tried to focus on the introductions, tried to focus on someone else other than Andrew, but as I was lifting my head up from another bow, I saw him.

He was there in the front row, in the last seat on the left. He was looking at me and smiling, mouthing, "Congratulations."

"And last but not least, our leading lady of the night and a new principle dancer here at NYCB—Aubrey Everhart!" The director said into the mic, and the audience cheered loudly.

"Miss Everhart?" She nudged me, whispering, "Miss Everhart, you need to take your final bow and leave the stage…"

I didn't move. I continued staring at Andrew.

"Miss Everhart?" She whispered, more harshly now. "Take a bow and get backstage…*Now…*"

I walked away from her and headed straight toward Andrew—taking my time down the stage's side steps. I stood in front of him, looking directly into his eyes—ignoring the confused murmurs of the crowd.

The director said a few more words, Mr. Ashcroft gave his regards, and the curtains closed without me.

As the audience gave one final applause and started to file out of the room, I finally found my voice.

"I thought you said you weren't coming…" I whispered. "Did you come here just to see my show or are you staying a little bit longer?"

"I'm staying a little bit longer."

"Does that mean permanently?"

"No." He wiped away my tears. "It means I'll stay here until you realize how terrible this city is—until you're ready to leave."

"I signed a contract for three years."

"Every contract is negotiable." He smiled and pulled me into his arms. "And if you don't apologize for ruining the closing credits tonight, they just might risk breaching it and fire you…"

"Where will you work?" I asked. "Are you going to practice law? *Can you* practice law?"

He kissed my lips. "I'll be teaching at NYU."

"What?" My heart immediately felt for the future students. "Why?"

"What do you mean, why?"

"You're a terrible teacher, Andrew...All of the interns at GBH hated you."

"I don't give a fuck."

"I'm serious..." I was actually worried. "I think you should reconsider. Teaching isn't for everyone, so—"

"First of all," he said, cutting me off and tightening his grip around me. "I *am* a good fucking teacher. It just depends on the subject matter..." He trailed his finger across my lips. "I can recall teaching you how to do something very well..."

I blushed.

"Second of all, last time I checked, all of the interns at GBH were quite unteachable and they were dumb as stones—all except one."

"The one that was a fucking liar?"

"Yes," he said. "That one."

"I heard she broke all your rules." I brought my hand up to his face. "I heard she ended your one dinner, one night, and no repeats streak..."

"I'm pretty sure that she didn't."

"Is that so?" I narrowed my eyes at him. "Is it still going on? Is that still your personal motto?"

"To a certain extent," he said, pressing his lips against mine. "Since I still like the sound of it, and will only be dating her from here on out, I'll just replace the word 'one' with '*more*'..."

epilogue

Six Years later…
New York, New York

Andrew

I stood in front of a classroom at New York University—counting down the seconds, asking myself why I'd ever agreed to this.

"Are there any questions?" I looked at my watch.

Several hands flew into the air.

"I'm only answering three of them." I pointed to a young woman in the front row. "Yes, you. What is it?"

"Um…" She blushed. "Good morning, Professor Hamilton. My name is—"

"I don't care what your name is. What is your *question*?"

"Um, it's been about two weeks since the semester started and you have yet to give us a syllabus…"

I ignored her and pointed to a jock in the back row. "Yes?"

"You also haven't told us what books we need to buy…"

"Does anyone in this classroom know the definition of the word, *question*?" I picked the last student, a redhead sitting by the window. "Yes?"

"Is it true that we're required to take turns bringing you coffee every day?"

I looked at the coffee mug on my desk, at the sign-in sheet that listed which student had brought it today.

"It's not a requirement," I said, picking up the cup. "But if you miss your day to bring me my coffee, I'll make sure everyone in this class regrets it."

They groaned collectively and shook their heads. A few of them still had their hands raised, but I was officially done for the day.

"Read pages 153 - 260 from the printout by next class. I expect you to know the ins and outs of each case. Class dismissed." I walked out, saying nothing further.

Slipping into my car, I noticed a new email on my phone.

Subject: Bathroom.
Thank you for sending me that very inappropriate note with my flowers today. Everyone in my cohort now knows that you and I have yet to fuck in our brand new bathroom.
Why are you so ridiculous?
—Aubrey.

Subject: Re: Bathroom.
You're very welcome for the flowers. I'm hoping that you liked them.
And that wasn't a "note" that I sent you. It's a demand that's about to be addressed within the next few hours.
Why do you deny that you love it?
—Andrew.

I could picture her rolling her eyes at my last message, so I revved up my car and sped back toward our home.

Even though I'd spent the last six years here, I was still building my tolerance for the things I once hated, things that now bothered me less and less, but I still had a long way to go.

Some memories can never be replaced...

Aubrey was completely captivated and entranced by this city, though. Whenever she wasn't incessantly touring with the ballet company, she was insisting that we try every restaurant, theater, and tourist attraction possible—trying to make me fall in love with everything again.

I parked in front of our brownstone—a newly purchased brick building in Brooklyn, and walked up the steps.

"Aubrey?" I said as I opened the door. "Are you in here?"

"Yes." She called from a distance. "And I'm not in the *bathroom*."

"You will be eventually." I walked down the hallway, stopping when I saw her hanging another frame in her office.

The walls were covered in pictures of her standing at center stage, a different picture for every night she'd opened a show.

"Do I need to have another room built for you and your photos?" I asked. "You're running out of space."

"No, I think this is the last one."

"Are you still retiring at the end of the month?" I stepped behind her and kissed her neck. "Or have you changed your mind yet?"

"I'm not changing my mind." She turned around to face me. "I think it's time for me to focus on something new."

"Becoming the female version of Mr. Ashcroft when you teach?"

"I won't be that bad," she said. "But I do need a break like you said, I think..."

I nodded. I'd been extremely supportive throughout her professional career—traveling with her out of the country to see some of the shows, hiring a personal massage therapist who was at her beck and call, and documenting all of her achievements from the newspapers.

But I'd recently noted a change—a shift, in her attitude: Although she was happy when she went to rehearsals, even happier when telling me about new things the company was trying, she seemed to be more interested in a life outside of the company, so I suggested that she take a short break.

I was still trying to figure out how she'd interpreted my suggested "break" as a "retirement."

"I loved dancing in Russia." She smiled, pointing to the picture. "Do you remember that?"

"I do remember that…" I said, continuing my assault of her neck, slipping my hand under her shirt.

She murmured as I rubbed my thumb around her nipple, as I gently bit her skin. But then she stepped away. "I actually need you to go fax my revised contract to the company…I have to let them know officially by five o'clock."

"*After* the bathroom." I clasped her hand. "We have four hours."

She rolled her eyes, but she gave in, taking my lead into the bathroom.

I turned on the water and pulled her dress over her head. "If you're hell bent on retiring from performing and simply teaching, we'll have more time to spend together."

"More time for you to convince me to leave New York?"

"We really don't have a reason to stay," I said, threading my fingers through her hair. "If you're going to teach, you can commute."

"And if I don't teach? If I decide to continue dancing instead?"

"I'll buy season tickets." I cupped her face in my hands, raising my eyebrow. "I never asked you to retire, Aubrey…I just think you need a break. You haven't taken a week off in more than six years…"

"I *am* going to take a break…"

"Is it going to last longer than two days?"

"A lot longer…"

"Two weeks?"

"It'll be at least nine months…"

"What?" I backed up, shocked. We'd stopped using protection once we moved in together, but she'd still taken birth control. "What are you saying, Aubrey?"

"I'm saying you're going to be a father," she said, nearly whispering. "And I think that's a good enough reason for us to stay…"

I was silent for several seconds, pressing my palm against her flat stomach.

"Are you okay?" she asked. "Is this not something that you wanted? I wanted to tell you this morning, but you were in a rush, so—"

I cut her off with a deep kiss and pulled her close, rubbing my hands against her bare back. "I'm more than okay…" I looked into her eyes. "It *is* something I wanted…"

She murmured, "I love you," against my lips and I said it back.

Breathless, she leaned against the shower door. "Can you go fax my letter now? It would really be nice if, for once, I wasn't late doing something because you have no self-control and were too busy fucking me."

"I'll definitely fax your letter…" I drew her lip into my mouth and squeezed her ass. "*After* the bathroom."

end of episode three

acknowledgments

WHOA. JUST WHOA.

This is probably going to be one of the most unprofessional author notes ever, but if you know me, you shouldn't be surprised. LOL.

Thank you Tamisha Draper for being there for me throughout my entire career—for pushing me to do my best each and every time, and for reminding me what's most important. I could never do this without you, and even though I'm sure your husband shakes his head at the forty times my name crosses your phone's screen a day, I'm happy you ignore him and still pick up. You are the best friend a girl could ever ask for, and I couldn't be more grateful that you've stuck by my side through all the good, the bad, and the utterly insane. I love you.

Tiffany Downs, OMG I'm so happy to have you back again. You are the balance—the perfect balance, and your support, advice, and friendship mean the world to me. Thank you for telling me that my "style" is just "my style" and that it's okay to be different.

Alice Tribue, OMG. OMG. THANK YOU for being my anchor in the sea of self-publishing. I had no idea that authors could be friends. No. idea. But I'm so happy to have someone like you who understands my version of crazy, someone who's there for me through thick and thin, and someone who actually thinks I don't suck. LOL

Keshia Langston, you are the most humble and honest author I know and I can't tell you how refreshing it is to know someone who just "gets" me, you know? #FLY HARD (Or as you would say…#FLYbitch LOL)

Brooke Cumberland, I'm sure I won't be winning any "book signing assistant of the year" awards and that I'm like the worst texter ever (Okay…There has to be someone worse than me… has to be LOL), but I want you to know that your friendship is invaluable to me. You are kind, thoughtful, compassionate, and even though you're crazy (Yes. You are crazy LOL), I wouldn't trade you for the world.

Laura Dunaway, even from afar, even thousands of miles away, I feel your support and love and I can't thank you enough for being there with me through it all.

Bobbie Jo Malone Kirby, I'm struggling with the words to write right now because how can I possibly say that I love you more than you'll ever know? That you believe in me more than I believe in myself, and that you keep me sane through it all? I am so damn happy that you walked into my life last year—still can't believe how seamlessly everything fell together, and now that you're here, you're mine forever and I'm never letting you go.

Natasha Gentile, thank you for being the crazy, nonstop emailing, nonstop *shut up Whitney and finish this book* person that you are. You're awesome inside and out, and I just might see you in Montreal soon…

Natasha Tomic, I'm utterly speechless at the amount of love and support you've shown to me and this series, for the magical strings you managed to pull while you were in NOLA back in May (THANK YOU), and for the heart filled messages you sent me when things were in disarray. I can't seem to find the proper phrasing that says, "I heart you big, I think you're incredible, and I'll never ever forget all you've done for me," so I will leave it at this…and then re-upload this book with the proper phrasing LOL

Nicole Blanchard, thank you for the teasers that saved my book. Literally. You have no idea how critical those were for RD1, and I'm so honored that you stepped in to be my PR/PA during this series when things were getting bigger than I could've ever imagined. THANK YOU.

Kimberly Brower, THANK YOU, THANK YOU, THANK YOU for reading this book over and over and helping me smooth out all of the flaws while I was losing my mind. You have no idea how much that means to me! You kept me sane during a very stressful time period, and I will never, ever forget that.

Thank you to all my friends, new and old, that I've made so far—Kimberly Kimball (You're going to kick ass this September, don't' worry), Stephanie Locke (I can't wait to meet you in St Louis, in person), Michelle Kannan (Did you catch your name in this? LOL), Lisa Pantano Kane (Thank you for reading everything, and I'm serious about that beta gig lol), & Lauren Blakely (You are my role model and you seriously inspire me more than you'll ever know…).

Thank you to every single blogger who promoted the hell out of this series and made it as successful as it became—to list a few, Milasy & Lisa at The Rockstars of Romance, Jenny & Gitte at TotallyBooked, Christine at Shh Mom's Reading, Nadine Colling at Hook Me Up Book Blog, Michelle Cole at The Blushing Reader Blog, Lori Economos at Sinfully Sexy, Tara and Tracie at Halos and Horns, Alison East at Three Chicks and Their Books, Hetty Rasmussen at BestSellers and BestStellars, Christine Cheff at Unhinged Book Blog, Miranda and Amie at Red Cheeks Reads, Cara Arthur at A Book Whore's Obsession, and COUNTLESS more! (Okay, now seriously…I *am* a scatter brain, so if I left you out, it wasn't intentional (I promise!), and since I self-published this, I can definitely add your name/blog and re-upload this book. LOL But seriously, though just tell me…)

Thank you to Evelyn Guy for the final proofing as always.

Thank you A MILLION TIMES OVER to Erik Gevers for stepping in to do the formatting. (Sometimes it's better to let a professional handle it LOL)

Thank you to my mother, LaFrancine Maria, for being there for me every step of the way, for making sure I keep everything in perspective, and for believing in everything I do. I LOVE YOU.

Last, and NEVER EVER least, THANK YOUUUUU to the best readers ever! You have made this Southern girl's dreams come true and I owe you everything! Yes, this is the last book for Aubrey & Andrew. Yes, I am known to change my mind but I think this one is sticking LOL. And no, no, no, I will not update their lives on my blog…just kidding. I totally will. I love you more than you'll ever know, and am grateful to have you aboard the F.L.Y. crew…

F.L.Y. (Fucking Love You)
Whit

43717751R00108

Made in the USA
Lexington, KY
10 August 2015